STEAL A KING

STELLA ANDREWS

NEWSLETTER

Sign up to my newsletter and download a free book

stellaandrews.com

STEAL A KING

Before you can see the light, you have to deal with the darkness.

I'm in danger and not just from my extremely handsome, cocky, billionaire captor.

It's surprising how quickly a normal life can unravel

Kidnapped on my way home from the airport, I was taken to him

Lucas Emiliano—the Casino King.

Tall, dark and handsome doesn't even begin to describe a man of extremes. A paradox, cruel and detached one minute and full of emotion the next.

Strong. Possessive. Dominant.

He wants answers and I'm going nowhere until he has them.

It turns out something was stolen from him. Something that earned me not just money but so much heat they sent a devil to guide me through the flames.

At times like this running is the only answer, but it appears he has other ideas. A King takes what he wants, and he wants me and I'm now his prisoner, locked in a gilded cage.

I don't want to be attracted to him, but I am and I don't want my heart to race and my body to shiver with desire when it sees him, but it does.

Then something happens that changes everything. Now it's not just about my survival, it's about much more than that. Will earning my freedom be a price I'm unwilling to pay?

Note to readers: If you like your books with a dark & delicious alpha male, hiding a sweet, domineering protective side. Meeting his match with an innocent, sweet, yet strong and independent female character who blows like a breath of fresh air through the pages - then this is the book for you.

A deliciously dark & captivating romance with so much steam & chemistry it burns.

The series is Five Kings, but each book can be read as a standalone and there are no cliff-hangers.

PROLOGUE

ELLA

his has been the best the day of my life and it was so easy. For the past ten minutes, I have done nothing but stare at the balance in my account. $200,000. How is that even possible?

Just thinking of what that money means to me, my family, our lives, gives me a warm feeling inside. It's done. It's over and hopefully now everything will work out. Mom will get the care she deserves and Hannah will have the lifesaving operation she badly needs.

Reaching for the phone, I make the call to give us our lives back and when I press 'end' it has taken just ten minutes to set the wheels in motion.

Silence is my only companion as I celebrate something that ends years of pain, worry and fear.

They will be ok.

The tears fall as I breathe out, and it's as if I've held that breath for three years. I feel so much emotion as I picture mom in Sunny Vale, the expensive home where the sick end their days surrounded by comfort and everything they could possibly wish for. I picture Hannah on her way to hospital in an ambulance that will deliver her the lifesaving operation she needs that we never had the resources to fund. They will be ok and all because of one small gold coin.

I must sit for close on two hours while I take it all in. The fact my struggle is over is difficult to comprehend because I never thought I'd reach this point and was fearful of making a different kind of journey where I tended two graves. Now I've delayed that a bit and it was worth every second of life I have given my family because just thinking of them leaving me is not worth considering.

The sunshine fades and is replaced by a different kind of light. Neon, fake and slightly ugly. The lights of Vegas. Intoxicating, provocative, deadly.

Many people come here seduced by what it can offer. They are reeled in on a promise that it will change their lives for the better. Gambling, wealth, luxury and sin. What happens in Vegas stays in Vegas, isn't that what they say? I hate it. I hate the cracks in the beautiful façade. I hate the greed and the fact that poverty exists under the glare of extreme wealth. One creates the other and rarely the other way around. People flock here with their cash and largely leave empty handed because the money stays and inflates the accounts of those who have it all figured out.

Making sure to check that everything is in order, I grab my purse and make to lock up a business that has provided my own kind of wealth. I bought into the whole Vegas vibe and offer a service that many can't replicate. Fake, counterfeit, smoke and mirrors. I will copy anything for anybody and charge accordingly. Most of the time it's documents, paintings, jewelry or personal items. Most things are legit, but it's the ones that aren't that make the most money. The under the counter jobs that pay my rent and bring hope for that one job that will change our lives forever. Today is that day because the coin was collected three hours ago and the money now lies in my bank account. Not for long though, because I have made arrangements to set the wheels in motion to make everything good.

Finally, we're getting somewhere.

Feeling upbeat, I grab my keys and turn off the lights and prepare to head home to pack.

As I hang the sign on the door, I can't quite believe I have this luxury.

Closed for three weeks

Tomorrow I'm heading home to visit my family. To sit with Hannah while she recovers from the heart operation that will make her life so different. To visit mom in her new home and make sure she's happy there. Take care of my family because I'm all they've got and make sure my money is well spent.

As I turn away from my business, I feel so proud. I have always been good at creating and through school and college was always in demand to copy things for my fellow students. It's what got me through - paid my way as I earned good money for my troubles. It was inevitable I'd make it my business and three years ago, Copycat opened its doors in a side street in Vegas and I have never looked back. The trouble is, it's an expensive place to set up, so the money never seemed to pile up fast enough for what I needed. That gold coin changed everything and now I've achieved my goal and can afford to take some time to make sure my family reaps the reward of my skill.

Yes, when I return in three weeks' time, everything will have gone according to plan.

CHAPTER 1

LUCAS

Two weeks later

I really need a break. It seems like everyone is pissing me off lately and this meeting is no exception. I am surrounded by fools and if I thought money brought you happiness; I was wrong.

"The problem is, the project is running behind and the costs are mounting up, making the investors worried. It's having a knock-on effect and now the press is questioning if it will ever get off the ground at all. Word on the street is you're pushing for something that will end up bringing you down…"

I raise my hand and the room falls silent as everyone turns to look at me. The man who spoke appears to be sweating and I know I make them nervous. Bill Bailey is my business advisor and a small part of me pities him for that but then again, I pay him well above the normal pay grade for his trouble so I snarl, "I don't care what they think, I only care about getting the job done."

My eyes flick to my chief of operations, Adam Remington, and a look passes between us. My brother from another mother, the man I trust with my life and the only person here I can stand to be in the company of for longer than sixty minutes. As always, he understands my mood and says shortly, "Meeting over, make it happen and next time we meet, make sure you come up with positive shit rather than dragging us down with your whinging and sniping."

I silently applaud his diplomacy because my trigger finger is itching to end this meeting in a more violent way because I am sick to the soul of the people who surround me. The men who profit from my business sense and the men who think they matter. They don't. Nobody matters. I have no loyalty, no love, and no emotion. I'm dead inside. The only thing that motivates me these days is money, and as the room empties, I reach for the cut-glass decanter behind me and pour two whiskies.

As the door clicks, I push one toward Adam and growl, "I was so close."

Chucking back the contents of the glass, I don't miss his amused grin and growl, "What?"

"You need to get laid. How long's it been?"

"Not interested."

Shaking his head, Adam finishes his drink in one and as I refill the glasses, he says with concern, "You may not want to but it will take the edge off. You can take your pick, hell I'll even play pimp for you, but something's got to give."

Despite myself, I laugh. "You'll play my pimp, interesting image."

He laughs. "It wouldn't be the first time because if I remember rightly, it was a regular thing back in the day. Business by day and whore by night, all engineered by yours truly."

"And now the beast has been tamed, and the bastard has

lost his partner in crime. Shouldn't you be getting back to her?"

At the mention of his wife, Penelope, Adam's eyes soften and I wonder what it's like—to find the one person you can't wait to see above all others. The one you would do anything for; the woman who completes you.

When Adam met Penelope, it changed him almost immediately. He only wanted her and I can see why. She has beauty, brains and a quick wit that impresses even me. He didn't hang around - we live in Vegas after all, and they were married inside six months. It suits me though because it keeps Adam grounded, focused on the business and after all, that's the only important thing in my life, anyway.

"Go, get the hell out of here, we'll sort this shit out in the morning."

"I can stay."

"Just fuck off, Adam, I've had enough of you for one day."

I laugh to take the edge off my words and he grins. "Then we feel the same."

I throw him my best death stare, but he just laughs and gathers up his belongings. "I mean it, Lucas, go and get laid because you're obviously doing a bad job of it yourself in your ivory tower with just your hand for company. Shall I send one of them up?"

"Only if you want a quick blow job before heading home to domestic bliss. I'll give you the two minutes you need before I leave."

He rolls his eyes and throws me the middle finger and leaves me festering in my own irritable shit.

By the time I make my way to my private elevator that takes me to my own floor of this sin palace I created, two hours have passed. This is normal for me. Business every hour I'm not sleeping. Maybe I should get laid, but I've grown weary of the whores, weary of the socialites on my arm that accompany me to business functions and shows. Meetings that require a plus one with the promise of a night in my bed and an expensive gift delivered the next day. I like the finer things, I always have, but sometimes a man needs a dirty whore to play with and yet, that no longer interests me. It's so meaningless, so degrading, and I feel as if I sell myself short every time I let a faceless stranger work my body just for a moment of pleasure that soon fades. No, I'm done with it, for now, anyway, because increasingly the only thrill I get these days is running my empire.

As soon as I step outside my private elevator, the hairs on my neck stand to attention. Call it a sixth sense, a premonition, but something is wrong.

I override the light sensor by pressing mute on my phone and reach for my gun.

A low chuckle tells me I was right and a hard voice says, "I'm impressed."

My hand eases on the gun and I say evenly, "To what do I owe this pleasure? I mean, it's always good to see you, but surely you could have called first."

Flicking on the light, I smile when I see the man sitting in the chair by the panoramic windows that have the whole of Vegas in view, and he stretches out and reaches for a glass of whiskey that sits on the table by his side.

"You alone?"

"Well, unless you count the invisible whores flanking me on every side, yes, I'm alone."

He nods and my curiosity pushes me further into the room.

"What's up?"

"I came to return something of yours."

"I wasn't aware I had lost anything."

"Are you sure about that?"

His tone is even but I sense an underlying threat behind it and once again my nerves stand to attention because pissing this man off is not on my agenda today—or ever for that matter.

"No, can't think of anything, maybe you should just cut the crap and tell me what you have that is so important it would drag you out here to ambush me in my own fucking apartment."

He laughs softly. "If you think this is an ambush, you have obviously forgotten who you're dealing with."

"I know who I'm fucking dealing with, which is why I'm being so civil."

I sit on the chair before him and reaching for a glass of whiskey that is never far away, say firmly, "So, cut the crap, what's the problem?"

He opens his hand and I stare at the gold coin in the palm of it and feel the tension increase.

"The coin, what happened?"

"You tell me."

"For fuck's sake, Ryder, cut the crap and just tell me already. I've had a shit day and the last thing I need is a riddle to solve when all I want is to sleep. Why are you sitting in my apartment with your fucking coin in your hand, showing me something that will only mean trouble?"

"I'm not."

I count to ten in my mind because this guy will be the death of me—probably literally and as I look at the grim reaper sitting opposite, I can tell he is seriously pissed off and I just hope I'm not the cause of it because if I am, I doubt I'll see the sun rise.

"This isn't my coin, it's yours—apparently."

"What?" I stare at him as if he's lost his mind and instinctively reach for my wallet.

As my fingers close around an identical gold coin, I sigh with relief. Pulling it out, I open my palm and we look at the two matching coins and then Ryder opens his other hand and I stare at a third in surprise.

"What's this?"

"My coin."

"Then whose is the other one?"

"Like I said, yours, apparently. It was found on a dead man in the Dragon's Ruin. Billy Channing and the last word on his lips was my name. Turns out I was framed for his murder and the person responsible came from here carrying your gold coin. So, forgive me for turning up unannounced, but what the fuck is going on?"

I have absolutely no words to answer him because I know nothing of this and yet this is Ryder King sitting here who will not just accept that and go away. I think fast because if someone has framed Ryder for murder in my name, I am in more trouble than I've ever been.

I study the coin in my hand and as much as it looks identical, there is something that doesn't feel quite right about it, so I say firmly, "May I?"

I take the coin from his hand and as I compare the two, I immediately know they are different from the weight alone. To anyone else they are identical, but to the trained eye they are poles apart and I hand them over to Ryder and say darkly, "Then we have a problem."

CHAPTER 2

ELLA

I'm not sure how I feel about coming back. Excited to be home, looking forward to getting back into business but missing my family already. It was good seeing them again.

Just seeing how happy mom is in her new home makes everything worthwhile. Hannah's operation is an apparent success, and she is recuperating at a facility giving her the nursing care she needs. She should be discharged in one weeks' time and can live a full and normal life. It felt good knowing I made that happen. She has a good prognosis, and the doctor thinks she will live a long and happy life and it's all down to my talent for copying things.

Now it's time to sort my own life out now the worry has gone, so I'm back to build a life that may even include finding someone to share it with.

As I join the line for the cabs, I drag my suitcase behind me. It does feel good to be back. The heat warms my soul and I have a spring in my step.

Even the jet-lag doesn't seem to bother me today, and I'm looking forward to the future for the first time in years.

Luckily, the line moves quickly and the cab driver takes my case and tosses it in the trunk while I slide onto the back seat.

Ten minutes and I'll be home, back in my apartment, back to the familiar and I'm looking forward to getting reacquainted with my comfortable bed.

The driver starts the engine and I say loudly, "Can you take me to the strip and I'll direct you from there?"

"Sure."

I settle back in my seat and close my eyes, grateful for the fact this is the last part of a long journey. To be honest, I'm looking forward to a long soak in the tub rather than sleeping in my bed because my sister only has a shower at her apartment and I've always loved the relaxation a hot and steamy bath gives me.

As I stare at the familiar landscape, it's almost as if I never went away and I wonder how much longer I'll be here. It's been on my mind to move nearer to Hannah; if anything, her illness had made me realize the importance of family and living here in Vegas is quite lonely really. I have friends, a select few who I unwind with at night, but I want more than that. A home, a family of my own and where better than near to my own.

Hannah has a boyfriend, Evan, who she's been dating for a couple of years already. They want a family and have been putting it off due to her condition. I know it's the most important thing to her, and I'm just hoping that it's now an option.

Sighing, I think on my own love life that's pretty pitiful, really. The guys that come here are after a good time mainly and don't stick around. Vegas is like that. A stopover destination. A fun weekend, or a vacation full of extremes. Any local guys get their pick of the tourists that flock here and life is one long party. No, I'm unlikely to find my soulmate in Vegas, so I must face the possibility of relocation sooner rather than later if I want my life plan to play out.

It doesn't take long before we hit the strip and I stare at the huge buildings that dominate the skyline. Plastic paradise. Gaudy, extreme, and a façade. A bright exterior to disguise the devastation within. Vegas is the queen of sleaze, and I live here.

Leaning forward, I say loudly, "If you aim for the university district, I'm not far from there."

He says nothing, which is a little odd and I'm surprised when he passes the exit.

"Hey, did you hear me, you missed the turning?"

He says nothing and I tap on the glass that separates us. "Excuse me."

Suddenly, I am thrown back in my seat as he takes a sharp turn and I stare in horror as he drives down a ramp into what appears to be an underground car park and immediately my heart beats faster and my senses move to high alert.

"What's going on, where are we?"

He screeches to a halt and I note the shutters come down behind us and I stare around me in fear. I'm in trouble, it's obvious this man is about to attack me and I'm the dumbass who made it easy for him.

Before I can say another word, he turns and says roughly, "Stop talking. If you value your life, you will do everything I say. Say nothing, do nothing, and come with me. If you try to escape, I will shoot you dead, got it?"

I'm in so much shock I just stare at him and he nods. "Get out of the car."

My fingers shake as I grasp the handle and as I step outside, I see two men approach. My knees almost give out on me when I see what's waiting because these men mean business, it's obvious. Dressed in leather and bad attitudes, their eyes tell me one false move and I'm dead. I have absolutely no choice but to follow them and despite the fact I try to act strong, I'm shaking inside.

The elevator is small when you are surrounded by three men who look as if they wrestle bears for fun. They look out of place in here, as if they've lost their way and ended up in the Twilight Zone. They are tough, crude and uncommunicative and I hardly even breathe for fear of recriminations. Through it all I hate myself because when did I get so weak? I should be screaming, trying to run, but where would I go? It's obvious the only way out of here would be in a body bag, so I have to trust my instincts and try to calm the fuck down because the first opportunity I get, I'm out of here.

Every floor we pass gives me thinking time as I wonder what's happening. Is it a trafficking ring; have I been kidnapped to be sold? I've heard of these things, or am I to be passed around like a toy at a rich man's party? It can only be that because I've done nothing wrong. I haven't upset anyone - at least I don't think I have. My mind is preparing me for the worst as a thousand images flash through it of what could be about to happen. I know this isn't going to end well - for me, anyway, and through the fear clouding my mind, I struggle to hold on to any hope left inside me.

The men beside me say nothing, and I daren't even ask. One false move could cost me my life and I kind of want to protect that, so I decide to say nothing and wait and see what's happening because this must surely be a case of mistaken identity; it can't be anything else.

The elevator comes to a sudden stop and my heart pounds inside me so hard it almost hurts. As the doors open, we step into a room that takes my breath away. I don't have time to appreciate the beauty of a place I have only seen in the movies, before I feel a hand against my lower back pushing me inside. The men step back into the elevator and as the doors close, they leave me alone and in the most trouble I have ever been in my life when I see the two men staring at me from across the room. My heart almost gives out on the spot because if Satan had twins, I'm looking at them.

CHAPTER 3

LUCAS

*N*ow she's here I'm not sure this was such a good idea. The woman looks fucking terrified and who can blame her? Ryder's plan is not sitting well with me, but this is our only hope. She's our only hope and so as his men shove her into the room, I'm the fucking idiot that's left to pick up the pieces.

Ryder says in his usual husky voice, "Sorry about this, darlin', I'll leave it to Lucas to fill you in on the reason you're here."

He turns to me and says darkly, "I'll be in touch."

As I watch him walk away, I feel the frustration tearing me up inside. Great, he gets to go, leaving me wallowing in a shit bath. He reaches the girl and whispers something in her ear and she bites her lip and blushes, shuffling on her feet, looking as if she is about to hurl herself through the floor to ceiling windows.

As the elevator door closes, I swear my last nerve follows him and I say tersely, "You should sit down."

I wave to the seat by the huge fireplace and pour her a

glass of brandy because she is going to need the whole bottle by the time I've finished with her.

She stands rooted to the spot and says nervously, "I think there's been a mistake."

"Why do you say that?"

"Because I don't think I'm the one you're looking for."

"I think otherwise, now sit."

My voice is curt and angry and to her credit she doesn't move a muscle and if anything takes a step backward toward the elevator.

"If you think you can escape, think again. That elevator runs on my command."

I wave the phone in the air and say bluntly, "The quickest way out of here is when I say so and I'll only agree when you tell me what I need to know, so take a seat, listen to what I have to say and give me what I need and then I'll arrange a ride home for you personally."

I hold out the glass and she eyes it suspiciously. "Relax, there's nothing in it but the alcohol needed to settle your nerves. Now, I haven't got all day and it's in your best interests to hear me out so we can get on with our day."

She nods and moves slowly toward me but waves the glass away with a terse, "I'm good thanks."

I place it on the table beside her. "You may change your mind about that."

"I won't."

She sits straight backed in her chair and looks as if she may snap at any moment.

"So, why am I here?"

Taking the seat on the other side of the fireplace, I open my hand and the look on her face when she sees the gold coin tells me we've hit the jackpot. She recognizes it.

"What can you tell me about this?"

17

She shifts a little on her seat and I watch her lower lip tremble and find it strangely fascinating to watch. Come to think of it, I'm having a hard time tearing my eyes from her because from the moment she stepped into the room, something shifted inside me. There is something enticing about this woman. Her hair is long and held back in a ponytail and her eyes are the deepest green. Her lips, that she appears to like the taste of, are plump and red and her figure would be the ruin of any man. She must be around 5ft 8 in flats and her long legs taper to a slim waist that disappears under a short denim skirt. Just dragging my eyes to that face is difficult enough because the tight t-shirt she's wearing certainly leaves nothing to the imagination.

Once again, she bites her lip and says nervously, "What do you want to know?"

"What can you tell me about it?"

"Not much."

Leaning forward, she says softly, "May I?" She reaches for the coin and as she takes it, my fingers brush against hers and she pulls them back quickly and says, "Is there a problem with it, it's just that, well, I don't do refunds?"

I can tell she's agitated, scared even, and I say roughly, "So, you made it."

"Yes." I see the concern in her eyes. There's something bothering her, and she says quickly, "I can offer you a credit against future purchases, but I'm afraid I no longer have the money."

She is trying so hard to keep control but I see the tears in her eyes and so I lean back and say harshly, "Who asked you to make this?"

"I don't know." She looks defeated which angers me and I say angrily, "So somebody paid you to make this coin and you don't even fucking know who, do you really expect me to believe that?"

"Am I in trouble?"

18

She looks so worried I shout, "Yes, you're in fucking trouble and you are not leaving until I get my answers, so start talking."

She reaches for the brandy and knocks it back in one go, and I smile to myself. I knew she'd need it. She shivers a little and is battling to hide her fear as she says softly, "I had a call one day, a few weeks back, from a man who asked if I could reproduce a coin. I told him I didn't counterfeit money, but he said it was no legal currency, just a theater prop. He would send me a picture and if it matched exactly, he would pay me well for a quick turnaround."

"How much?"

She inhales sharply and her voice quivers as she whispers, "Two hundred thousand dollars."

I stare at her in shock. Two hundred thousand dollars. What the fuck? She starts to tremble and says weakly, "Was it illegal?"

I should put her out of her misery and reassure her, but how can I? I know nothing, so I say softly, "Where did you send it?"

"I didn't. A woman came to collect."

"Do you have her contacts?"

"No."

"Does your shop have CCTV; can we access it?"

"No."

I exhale sharply. "So, you took two hundred thousand dollars from a customer who you didn't meet and then handed the order over to a woman who you have no way of getting back in touch with. Are you stupid?"

She raises her eyes and I see a little of the fire return as she says roughly, "Don't you insult my business practices. I see all kinds of people in my shop and none of them fill out a questionnaire. I took an order; I made the product, and a woman collected. The money was placed in my account and that was it. The reason it was so expensive was on the under-standing the transaction was a ghost one. No repercussions, no comeback, and how was I supposed to know it was dodgy? I've done nothing wrong, so if you'll excuse me, I've had a very tiring day and need to go home."

"About that."

She looks up and I shrug. "You go home when I tell you. As soon as we've found who your customer was, the better for you, so until we have all the information, you stay with me."

"You can't do that!"

She stands quickly and I lean back in my chair. "I can and I will. That coin you made has set off a chain of events that's out of control. Two people are already dead because of it, the man who received the coin and the woman who collected it."

She sits down heavily and whispers, "Oh my god."

"So, listen to me if you value your life. Until we know who we're dealing with, you're not safe. Your family is not safe and *I* am not safe. I need you to stay here by my side until we work out who ordered it, who paid the money and why and until all the puzzle pieces fit, you're going nowhere."

CHAPTER 4

ELLA

I'm in way out of my depth. Just being here tells me that. The men that brought me and the ones they delivered me to. These men don't play by the rules, hell they probably don't know what a rule is. Seeing them was bad enough, but when one of them whispered to me, I felt my knees almost give way.

"Lucas Emiliano is not a nice man, don't piss him off."

Those were his exact words, and he didn't need to add the rest of the sentence to the name. I know who Lucas Emiliano is, hell the whole of Vegas has it imprinted on their brain because if you mess with the Casino King, you disappear, probably to the bottom of the Grand Canyon.

I almost can't concentrate because just being in the same room as him is messing with my mind.

He's angry. I could tell that on sight.

He's got a short fuse, that's common knowledge, and I'm in the firing line.

Lucas Emiliano is not titled the Casino King for nothing. He owns the corporation that awards gaming licenses. He controls the whole casino empire, regardless if he owns them or not, and most of them he does. He is the top dog in the gambling world and I've angered him.

He was right, I did need that brandy because I'll be lucky to get out of here at all, judging by the anger in his expression and the look in his eye. It doesn't help that he is the most attractive man I have ever laid eyes on. Dark hair cut close and dark smoldering eyes. His shirt is rolled up at the sleeves revealing a splash of ink and his muscles ripple as he moves, revealing that working out is one of his hobbies. There is something so primitive in my reaction to Lucas Emiliano, and despite the fact I'm well out of my depth here, he fascinates me for all the wrong reasons.

Then there's the money. He can't lay claim to that if he's not my customer, so I relax a little. But then who is the person who made the order? I feel like such a fool when I realize I have no way of knowing. I let greed blind me to anything but taking the money and making sure my family was safe. What if the cops come calling and seize my assets? I could go to prison and I'm drowning in fear because I know nothing of this world they live in.

"Just breathe, Ella."

His words shock me back into the room and I whisper, "You know my name."

"I know your name, your address, your age and what you have for breakfast. I know you went to school in Pittsburgh and moved to North Carolina when you were nine. I know you have a sister and a mother who's dying of cancer. I know your sister has a heart condition and has just undergone surgery to save her life. Your favorite color is blue and you hate cruelty to animals. You're 24 years old and own the Copycat store in town. Need I go on?"

My mouth drops open but no words come out and he shrugs, "I like to know who I'm dealing with. There's not a lot I don't know about you Ella Quinn, but I'm guessing you know shit about me."

"I know you."

He raises his eyes and I say quickly. "They call you the Casino King. You own this town and run the gambling operations in all other States. Your reputation makes people curious; they whisper about you and what you are capable of. They are fascinated by the world you inhabit and speak of you in hushed tones. You are considered a player, a bastard and a man with no morals. Probably someone who kicks puppies and turns charities away unless there's something in it for him. Women want you, men want to be you and most are warned off you. Yes, Mr. Emiliano, I know about you and your reputation was enough to tell me I wasn't interested in finding out anything more."

To my surprise, he laughs softly. "Is that right?"

"What part?"

"The part where you're not interested."

"Yes. What's the matter, can't you understand that not everyone wants a man like you in their life?"

"Not really."

He smiles and laughs softly. "I haven't met anyone yet who doesn't want what I can give them."

"That doesn't mean they *like* you, Mr. Emiliano, it just means they use you - big difference."

I think I've gone too far when his eyes flash and he turns away and for a moment I think he's contemplating putting the gun to my head that I see tucked inside his jacket on the back of his chair.

Then he says in a low voice, "Don't you think I know that. That the people I surround myself with are here for what I can give them and what I can do for them?"

I say nothing and he turns and raises his eyes, "Well, don't you?"

"If you're asking, it must be true."

He nods. "You make a good observation, I like that. Anyway, none of these observations matter because we are stuck together until circumstances dictate otherwise. I wasn't kidding when I told you that. You are now my guest, prisoner, call it what you like, but you go nowhere outside this apartment unless I say so."

"You really meant that, but why? I mean, I have a business to run, a life. By all means come back with me and I'll give you what I have, show you my records, anything to put your mind at rest that I'm not involved in whatever this weird shit is that's going on. But please, let me go back home, I'm begging you."

"Interesting."

"What is?"

He smirks and runs his eyes across my body in a lazy way that has me squirming inside. "I like a woman who begs."

"I'm guessing you do; most men like you would."

"What man is that?"

I know he's playing with me, so I snap, "A man who gets his kicks from intimidating women, men, and anything else that catches his attention. A man with more money than morality who thinks it buys him the right to do what the fuck he likes. Take me, case in point. You think you can control me, keep me here because of business I have no part in. Well, I am my own person and not impressed by men like you, and I demand to leave immediately before I report you to the cops for false imprisonment."

My chest heaves as I lay it all out there, and if anything, I'm proud of myself for making a stand. I've been reasonable, despite the fact he virtually kidnapped me, but it appears my words have fallen on deaf ears because he shakes his head.

"Request denied. Now sit there, shut up and listen to what

I'm about to say because if you won't do this for me, or for you, then do it for your family."

"What do you mean?" The fear hit me as soon as he mentioned my family and he says curtly, "I wasn't lying when I said they would be in danger, so here's what's happening. You are my only link to the person who has caused two deaths already and will think nothing of clearing away anyone that can direct us to him. Your family is now involved because you visited them and may have told them something. I have arranged a guard on them so you should be grateful for that because all the time you're with me you're safe. If you return home, to work, you are a target. The person who ordered that coin had a plan that hasn't worked out. He or she will know we're onto them, which may make then careless. Nobody is safe until we discover their identity, so cut the attitude, save the smart remarks and accept that we are stuck with each other for however long this takes. So, your case is in your room, I suggest you make yourself at home while we wait for Ryder to unravel the facts."

"Ryder?"

"The man who just left. He is currently sifting through every part of your life and business to find the trail that will lead us to your elusive customer, so relax and enjoy your stay in the most expensive prison in the world."

He stands and says tersely, "Follow me, we've done enough talking."

He strides from the room, leaving me to follow, and I know in my heart he's right. I need to believe what he said because if my family is in any danger at all, I owe it to them to see this through. What that means for me, I'm not sure but surely it will only take them one day, two at the most, so I can cope with that, surely. I mean, how hard can it be?

CHAPTER 5

LUCAS

I lied to her. As I walk from the room, I laugh to myself. I told her she was safe. She's not—from me. I love a woman with attitude. Someone who's not afraid to answer back; a woman with balls of steel who isn't afraid to stand up for what she believes in. Then there's the soft, vulnerable side to her that makes me want to protect her. The shivering woman who I know would feel good in my arms. But it's the fire in her that excites me the most. Those long legs wrapped around my waist as I drive in deep. The full and plump lips that would look good wrapped around my cock and those tits that would replace a good meal for me any day of the week. Yes, Ella Quinn is not safe from me because I have been searching for a woman like her and she will only leave when I'm done with her.

She follows me to one of my guest rooms that I had made ready today. When Ryder discussed the plan with me, I was dreading every minute of having a stranger invading my personal space. I hate entertaining people here. Hell, I have an empire of hotels and don't think I've ever allowed anyone to spend one night as my guest, let alone several, preferring instead to entertain them in one of my many penthouses dotted around the city and the states. Now I'm even more surprised to find I'm looking forward to it. There is something so refreshing about Ella Quinn. An innocent aura that would look good broken at her feet when I ruin her forever. A perfect Angel, untarnished and innocent, realizing how much better it is to be ruined and corrupted.

Yes, today is not turning out as bad as I thought it would, and hearing her soft footsteps behind me and the waft of fear that surrounds her, is turning me on so much I'm tempted to move this on tonight. Then again, that would probably scare her, which is not what I'm about. I prefer a gradual awakening, a discovery on her part, that moment when she falls - hard and breaks open at my feet, her inner devil stepping out from the remnants of respectability, knowing that I'm the one responsible. Too bad that's the moment I usually kick them out. I lose interest at that point and move onto the next. Yes, Lucas Emiliano is a bastard and I wouldn't have it any other way.

We reach the furthest room from mine and if I wanted, she could live here and I wouldn't see her for days. That was my intention anyway, but as I open the door and hear her soft gasp behind me, I'm wondering about moving her a little closer. Just thinking of her lying in the next room to me would be delicious torture, knowing she was so close yet so unattainable would be the biggest turn on—for me.

"This room is…"

She can't even find the right adjectives to use, and I congratulate myself on attracting the best designers that money can buy. Because yes, this room is impressive by anyone's standards, and to my knowledge she is the first person to ever see it.

Her rather shabby suitcase is set up on the stand and looks like a blemish on alabaster skin. Ella herself sticks out much the same in her scruffy clothes as she looks around with travel weary eyes. Yet she has a natural beauty that dims the effect of the extreme wealth around her. Like a freshly bloomed wild flower in an award-winning garden, it is her that draws the most admiration.

I make a fist because I am fighting the urge to touch–her. Release that long luscious hair from the binding, watch her shiver as I run my fingers down her perfect face. Watch her bite her lip and her eyes glaze over with lust before I rid her of her clothes and run my eyes over nature's finest piece of art.

Instead, I turn away and say gruffly, "This is your room, not bad for a prison but remember that's exactly what it is. You will live here until the matter is resolved. We have your phone, your personal items, passport, money and credit cards, where I have placed them in my safe. There is no way out of here unless I agree. Your meals will be served to you here, and you have full use of the facilities of any door that remains unlocked. Once again, I have control of that, so if I don't want you in a particular room, you will not be granted access. There is a private gym, a pool on the terrace and a cinema room. If you would like a massage, or a beauty treatment, you can call reception and arrange it—the list of what's on offer is beside your bed. I will check in with you when I have anything to say, I may need to ask some questions to help resolve this situation and then, when that happens, you will be taken home safe in the knowledge you are alive at least. Any questions?"

"What about my family?" She sounds nervous and afraid, and it's obvious they mean the most to her. Many women I know would be thinking only of themselves at this point, yet my little wild flower is full of concern for others—I love that about her.

"They are being protected, but they won't know. Ryder

runs a slick operation and has eyes on them 24/7. He is also working on building the picture that led up to this, to find the person responsible for daring to think they can step into our lives and leave at will. No, you leave your family's safety to the professionals and know you're safe here."

"Am I?" She stares at me with an unwavering gaze and I laugh to myself. "Probably not, which is why I intend on keeping my distance."

I feel a flash of disappointment when I see the relief in her expression which surprises me. Why do I care if she wants to spend time with me or not? She's a stranger, a slightly scruffy girl off the street, one I wouldn't give a second look to if I saw her pass me one day. She is beneath me in every way and above me in the ones that count. She looks around her as if she's fascinated but given half a chance would change everything for something simpler, less ostentatious, less like a show home and more like a real one—whatever that looks like.

Fighting an incredible urge to see her naked, I look down and say brusquely, "I'll leave you to settle in. Enjoy your stay, Miss. Quinn, for both our sakes, I hope it's not a long one."

I don't even wait for her answer, I don't even take the time to show her around because I need air and fast because the stench of innocence is burning my soul. I don't want the responsibility of her. I don't need it. I have an empire to run, I have meetings, emails, business dinners, trips and an endless round of shit to deal with but strangely the only thing I want to do—is her.

CHAPTER 6

ELLA

*A*s soon as he leaves, I want him back. I'm not sure at what point I lost my mind because I should be dancing for joy that's he's gone and I'm unharmed because one look into those eyes and I know I'm in trouble. I've never met a man like him before. Hard, ruthless and dangerous, wrapped in a packaging that any woman would be happy to discard. I should be happy this isn't what I feared. That I was to be used for a man's pleasure, then murdered, or worse. Ordinarily this is a dream come true, an adventure of the most decadent kind.

I look around in shock and like a kid in a candy store, my eyes shine with greed. This place is a palace and he is the king. I am in no doubt about that because Lucas Emiliano oozes authority. He could have snapped his fingers and I would have done anything – I really mean that because men like that aren't from this world – my world, anyway and yet one taste would ruin me forever. I'm not stupid enough to think any different, so perhaps it's a good thing he's intent on keeping his distance because that will take away any temptation to do the wrong thing – as I always seem to do.

Now I'm alone I'm keen to explore. A prison he says, well throw away the key and sentence me to life because I am in heaven in this room alone.

I HAVE NEVER SEEN SO much luxury and this room would fit my whole apartment and my neighbours either side. It's like an apartment in itself because it appears to be made up of several interconnected rooms. Everything seems brand new, from the velvet covered chairs, to the art on the walls. The drapes are weighted silk and the floor feels good against my feet with its cream shagpile carpet.

I set about exploring a decadent paradise. From the floor to ceiling windows overlooking the resort hotel. The whole of Vegas lies like a magic carpet beneath my feet yet there is not a sound to be heard. Each room reveals another surprise and the best one of all is the bedroom because I could live in this room alone. The emperor sized bed is dressed with white bedding with not a crease in sight. The cushions stand to attention and the smell alone is divine. Floral scents mix with freshly washed linen and after the journey I've had it's a place I plan on getting acquainted with real soon.

Before that a soak in the tub beckons and I open the door to bathroom Utopia and I do actually scream with delight when I see the huge roll top bath facing the window overlooking the skyline because you could have a party in this bathroom and invite several guests.

There appears to be everything I need, so I set about running a deep bath and make sure to use the array of products on offer. There are warm towels heating on the rail and a large robe folded on the table to the side. Nothing is more important to me right now than this bath and I don't even care that I'm technically a prisoner. I know that should bother me, hell I should be looking for ways to escape because I've only got Lucas's word that I'm safe. Well, he can do what he likes as long as I spend one night in heaven first because this is now officially the best day of my life.

I think I now hold the record for the longest time spent in a tub in history because it must be two hours later that I finally leave, wrapped in my robe and venture into the room. As I slip under the covers of the largest bed I've ever been inside, my eyes grow heavy. I need to sleep so badly and even though I haven't eaten for several hours, it's not as important as sleep, so it's with a groan I drag myself out of it when I hear a tentative knock on the door, followed by movement outside in the living room.

My heart quickens when I imagine Lucas has returned and yet I'm surprised at the flash of disappointment I feel when I see a man setting out food on a table beside the window.

"Oh, um, hi."

He straightens up and looks around with interest and his mischievous grin puts me at ease immediately.

"Well, hi, honey, just look at you all ready for bed already. This is Vegas baby; we sleep when we're dead."

Despite how strange this all is, I smile as he winks. "I'm Tom, as in Cruise but without the game, although god knows my plan is to marry that man one day and share every delicious bit of him, including his name."

He laughs and I shake my head and giggle as he looks at me with interest.

"So, Lucas told me you'd be his guest for a few days. I must say I was surprised."

"That's two of us."

"Well, whatever the reason, you don't have to worry, honey, that man is rarely here, anyway, it's more my home than his."

"Oh, so you live here too."

"I wish."

He laughs. "No, I'm just the hired help; you know, chief slave but he pays well and keeps out of my way mainly, although god knows I'd do anything for that man if he asked and I mean anything, if you know what I mean, although sadly he prefers the female of the species."

He holds out the chair with a flourish.

"Come and sit, princess and just look at the delicacies the chef has prepared. Lucas pinched him from the Ritz in London and I must say, despite the fact he's so rude and obnoxious, he's instantly forgiven when he serves up magic like this."

I hastily head over because the smell alone is enough to have me groaning out loud and Tom fills a glass with water and says dutifully, "Do you have a wine preference?"

"Oh, um white would be lovely."

"Any particular brand, we have them all?"

"Whatever you think."

"Then allow me to corrupt you forever and serve up one of the most expensive on the menu."

I feel a little worried because I may have to pay for that and he must notice it because he laughs softly. "While you're here make sure you take everything on offer and I mean everything." He winks. "Lucas treats his guests well and they have their pick of anything they want, all completely gratis, so make the most of it while you can."

His enthusiasm settles any nerves I have because this must be above board and the fact he knows I'm here guarantees my safety, surely.

As he finishes up, he looks with satisfaction at the feast meticulously arranged in front of me and says quickly, "Ok, I should leave you in peace. I'll be back to clear away and if you can think of anything you need, ask me and your wish will be my command."

"Oh, don't go, can't you sit with me?" I'm not sure where that came from and he looks surprised. "Goodness, angel, of course I couldn't. Whatever would Lucas say if he found us enjoying a cosy chat. No, despite my manner - I know, I really should have paid more attention at servant school - I would never overstep my position. Why do you ask?"

"I suppose I'm a little lonely and thought you could fill me in on how this place works, you know, tell me what I need to know and maybe a little about, um, Lucas."

It feels wrong saying his name as if he's a personal friend of mine and Tom shakes his head sadly. "Sorry, honey, I can't tell you one word about my employer, it's more than my job's worth. I'm guessing you will just have to rely on google, it's usually a good friend to me and tells me everything I want to know. My job is to serve you food, drink, fetch you whatever you want, but you can't leave."

The sympathy in his eyes makes me wonder what Lucas told him about me – this situation and the reason I'm here at all. Once again, I feel a little weird about this whole set up and despite the luxurious surroundings, feel a pang of longing for my small but completely safe apartment that I left three weeks ago. Then my thoughts turn to mom and Hannah and I know they must be worried that I returned safely. What if they called my phone, or left a message at my apartment? They will worry if I don't reply, so I say quickly, "I don't suppose you could arrange for me to call my mom? Let her know I returned safely."

Tom looks worried. "I'll see what I can do, honey, leave it with me. Anyway, I really should go, you know, things to do and people to, well, do actually."

He laughs softly and this time as he turns to leave, I don't stop him. Just the look in his eyes told me he knows I'm a prisoner here. I wonder what Lucas told him, does anybody else know? What if they think I'm one of his whores? Julia

Roberts from Pretty Woman, secreted inside the Beverly Wilshire because Edward was paying her. Just thinking of the similarities in how it looks makes me burn with embarrassment. Maybe I'll use this time to work out a plan because no man tells me what I can and can't do and it's time to make a stand – but not until after I've eaten this amazing food and spent the night in a suite of rooms fit for a queen.

Yes, he just caught me in a weak moment, so I need to build up my strength for the fight that lies ahead.

CHAPTER 7

LUCAS

*a*dam looks worried, and yet the new resort is the furthest thing from my mind today. Usually, I'm all about the business. Nothing distracts me from that, but there's something much more interesting hijacking my thoughts today and I wonder what she's doing now.

It feels strange thinking of her in my apartment—a place that stands empty for most of the time. A soulless void filled with expensive toys but lacking the life that makes a person want to spend time there—until now.

I am weirdly fascinated by Ella Quinn. Just leaving her to get on with it while we wait for Ryder to unravel the mystery should have been the easiest part of the plan. I could even visit one of my other Casinos; take a trip out of State to check on the rest of my empire. It would be so easy to do except for one thing–I don't want to.

Adam is staring at me with a look on his face I know only too well, and I sigh. "Spit it out."

"What's up?"

"You tell me, that's what I pay you for."

"I'm not talking about the business, hell we know what's definitely up there but you."

"Me?"

"Yes." He stares at me with an intensity I'm used to, but today it just irritates me.

"As I said, spit it out."

"You seem distracted, did something happen last night?"

"No."

I shrug because the plan is that nobody knows about Ella and her business. Ryder is shady like that. Need to know basis and all that and the only people that know she's even here are, Tom, my personal chef and Dixie, my assistant. The fact I scare the shit out of them ensures their loyalty, plus the fact I pay them more per month than they would usually earn in a year keeps their eyes lowered and their lips firmly shut. Ryder has his operatives acting as security and so I need to offer no explanations and yawn.

"You do the worrying enough for both of us. So, good news, you get to do it alone today because I'm heading upstairs."

The look on Adam's face makes me smile because I never 'head upstairs' when there's business to attend to and he shakes his head. "Fine, but whatever it is that you're hiding, I hope it's worth keeping from your most trusted friend. You really know how to hurt a guy's feelings."

He places his hand on his heart and makes a face, and I grin.

"You'll live. What can I say, shit happens, people move on."

Shaking his head, he snaps his computer shut and pushes back from the table. "I just hope it's a woman because you need to get laid my friend and you don't need a shrink to tell you that's your biggest problem right now."

"You think I have a problem getting laid?"

I laugh softly and he nods. "Yes, actually—I do because it's obvious you're searching for more than meaningless sex right now, or Tom has finally got his way and you're battling with the closet door."

He grins and heads off before I can retaliate, and I'm glad to see the door slam behind him. Business is the furthest thing from my mind today because of her. If I'm struggling with anything, it's that.

I head to the elevator that leads to my private apartment and Dixie follows me, speaking in hushed tones. "Lucas, your 2.30 has arrived in reception, should I show her to the boardroom?"

Thinking about the journalist who has badgered me for months for an interview, makes me irritable. The last thing I need is bad press right now and if I turn her away, I'm causing more trouble for myself than necessary.

Dixie looks worried because as always, she's the one who has to deal with the fall out of my decisions and I shake my head angrily.

"How long can you stall her?"

She looks anxious. "I can't. Right after that meeting you have one with the architect. He's probably on his way as we speak and needs an answer by close of business today to sign off the plans."

My world crowds around me like pressure in the deepest part of the ocean and where I usually thrive on it. Today I wish I could just walk away—but I can't.

Sighing, I say roughly, "Just give me thirty minutes. Show her to the boardroom and get her a drink, snack whatever the fuck she likes. Make sure she's happy, give her a tour, anything, just let me have a moment to pee for Christ's sake."

The elevator waits and I step inside, leaving an unhappy assistant behind. Dixie will do as she's told, and I don't think I could function without her. She's worked for me for five years and weathered the storm much better than most, so I'm a little kinder to her, treat her well, remember her birthday, Christmas and spoil her from time to time. It helps that's she not attracted to me because most of my assistants have done everything they could to end up in my bed, but I'm not interested. I never am—until now.

Thirty minutes is long enough for a quick fix, maybe long enough to drive her from my mind, so I can carry on doing what I do best - making money.

The apartment is quiet as usual when I step inside and I listen keenly for any sound indicating where she is.

I head toward her suite of rooms, feeling weird about this whole thing. I'm not even sure what I'm going to say to her and need to think up an excuse and fast because I'm walking into unfamiliar territory here and it's not welcome.

I hear the noise of a television coming from the living area of her room and I knock sharply and head inside.

The sight that greets me makes this whole trip worthwhile because Ella is bent over with her ass in the air following some sort of instruction on the screen as she joins a fitness class.

My cock stirs when I see her perfect ass covered in nothing but a very short pair of shorts and the vest clinging to her tells me there's nothing underneath but what nature created in her finest moment.

Her hair is up in a messy heap on top of her head and I hear her groaning as her breathing comes hard and fast.

Leaning against the door, I appreciate the show and as she straightens up, she catches sight of me out of the corner of her eye and steps back in shock.

"What the…"

The shock on her face makes me smile, but the sight of her nipples poking against the drenched fabric of the vest makes my cock jump with delight as she says angrily, "Don't you knock?"

"Maybe I did."

"Obviously not loud enough."

I can tell she feels uncomfortable and reaches for a towel on the floor beside her, giving me another opportunity to stare at her cleavage.

As she straightens up, she wraps it around her and snaps, "Have you come here to say I can leave, is my cab waiting?"

"No and no."

I move into the room and notice she backs off a little, her eyes wide and her face flushed.

Fixing her with my darkest look, I say gruffly, "I have some questions."

"Oh, um, well, I'll try to answer them, but I'm not sure if I can add anything to my earlier statement."

"Statement." I laugh softly, "I'm not the fucking cops, Ella, no, I have some questions but I don't have long. I came to tell you to expect to have dinner with me at 7 sharp. Meet me in the dining room and dress for dinner."

"The dining room?"

"Two doors down on your right."

"You mean here, in your apartment, I thought we would be going out."

"You thought wrong. As I said, you're my prisoner, and that doesn't include going on dates with the one holding the key to your ball and chain."

"Doesn't it?" She shakes her head and fixes me with an equally dark look. "Well, as you're not the cops, by your own admission and I haven't actually legally been detained and as you have no jurisdiction here, I'd say that labels you as my kidnapper, so if anyone's going to prison around here, it's you."

She stands with her arms crossed which only pushes her

tits together making me even harder if that's possible and says angrily, "So, if you want my full cooperation, for me not to press charges when you return me to my normal safe life, then you will not treat me like a caged animal and think of me as a human being on the same level as you. A person with feelings and needs. A woman who is going silently mad with no company to speak of and no idea of what the hell is going on. I asked your assistant for a phone to call my mother. Even a prisoner gets one call at least, so hand me your phone, I demand it."

"You. Demand. It."

My voice is low and threatening and I know she hears the threat in it because she turns a whiter shade of pale and steps back even further. Once again, she bites that fat lip and I'm blinded with lust for this wild creature who is so sexy I'm having a hard time thinking of anything but her on her knees sucking my cock.

I make toward her and she says fearfully, "What are you doing?"

I say nothing and as she backs away, I invade her space until her back is pressed against the wall. She looks up at me through fearful eyes that cause the blood to run like a raging rapid through me, and as I lift my hand and push it against her neck, I love the fear in her beautiful eyes as they swim with terror.

CHAPTER 8

ELLA

hat have I done? I went too far, I'm an idiot and completely mad because I should have paid heed to the rumors. *Lucas Emiliano is not a nice man.* Hell, even the man with him told me that confirming every other whisper I've ever heard about him.

Now he's so close I can hear him breathing as he pins me to the wall with one hand and stares at me through those dark, deadly eyes.

I want to close my eyes to shut out the inevitable that's coming my way, but I can't. It's as if this man fascinates me. It's like watching a snake the moment before it strikes. I am frozen in fear, strangely detached from the situation as I look on with interest to see what happens next. Will he snap my neck in two with those strong hands? Press a thumb hard against my skin to cut off my air supply? Will I regret the moment of madness when I allowed my voice to seal my fate?

I can almost taste his scent, its potent, musky, swirling with pheromones and my knees are so weak it's a good thing he's holding me up. Despite it all, I feel a wet trail of desire filling my panties which shocks me more than anything.

I want him.

This violent, damaged man who scares the hell out of me. I want him so badly I start to shiver with desire and as his lips crash against mine I am so shocked I let him in. He punishes my mouth by nipping on my lip, and I taste my own blood. His tongue plunders mine and binds it to his and I feel him hard against me, the thin fabric of my workout clothes doing little to protect me as he pushes in hard and swallows me whole. There is now nothing in my life but him. He is all around me, against me and inside my mind. I should be scared, cowering in fear, but I am so turned on I can't think straight.

His low growl causes my heart rate to increase as I feel the hunger inside him for me. His hold lessens against my neck and instead he wraps those hands behind my head and pulls me closer, devouring my lips and extracting my self-esteem.

I want him. I want him so much if he tore my clothes off, I wouldn't care. If he took me right here against this wall, I would consider it the best day ever. Instead, he pulls away and stares deep into my eyes and growls, "Just for the record, next time you demand something from me, next time you raise your voice in anger—against me and next time you throw my hospitality back in my face, it won't be my kiss you feel. I will bend that ass across my lap and spank you so hard you won't sit down for a week. You will beg me to stop and guess what—I won't. So, carry on with your day and meet me at 7 in the dining room, dressed appropriately. I will not ask a third time. If you refuse, you will be confined to a different room where I hold the people who piss me off and that, my wild flower, is the opposite to luxury. So, it's your choice, you play by my rules, or we play a different game."

He drops me and my fingers instinctively go to my neck as I gasp for air. He says nothing and just turns away and walks to the door, but before he leaves, snaps, "You can call your mother tonight if I am pleased with you. Rewards are earned around here—not demanded. Learn from that."

He leaves me reeling, and as soon as he leaves it's as if a black cloud goes with him and as I fall to the nearby chair, I struggle to make sense of what just happened. He was so violent, he changed in the blink of an eye and I never saw it coming.

His reputation is well earned because he is definitely not a nice man.

Then why do I want more?

MY AFTERNOON IS SPENT WORRYING about what will happen later on. After a long shower where I tried to remove the imprint of his touch, I stare at my possessions with frustration. I have nothing to wear. Nothing suitable for a meal with a gazillionaire. The smartest thing I own is a peasant style white dress that is more suited to the beach than an evening dinner date.

Then there are my shoes, I only have sneakers and one pair of strappy sandals. I'm going to look ridiculous and I briefly wonder about tearing down the silk drapes and hand stitching a dress somehow because this is a disaster.

My nerves are in full control of my body as I sit rocking on the chair in the corner of the room, desperately trying to think of an alternative because just thinking of what punishment awaits me if he's displeased, causes me to hyperventilate with fear. It's bad enough fearing physical injury, but what is this other place he's talking about? I'm under no illusions it's not as palatial as the room I'm in now and I will do anything to stop myself from experiencing that dubious pleasure.

I can't even eat any of the food Tom brought up when I was in the shower. It all sits under the silver domes on the side because just the sight of it will be enough to make me hurl.

A loud knock on the door brings my mind back from the abyss and I say shakily, "It's ok, you can come in."

I expect to see Tom, here to collect the tray, but instead I see a tiny woman staring at me with curiosity. She looks to be in her late thirties and is wearing a smart suit with her skirt dusting just above her knees. She has her hair slicked back in a ponytail and her make-up is impeccable.

She looks as if she's involved somehow because she doesn't seem surprised to see me, and as I jump up, I notice she is carrying what looks to be a garment bag.

"Miss. Quinn, I'm Dixie, Lucas's assistant. He has instructed me to arrange a suitable dress for this evening. I believe you are joining him for dinner at 7pm sharp."

She nods to emphasize her point and I know she's rein-forcing the time, which makes me fearful all over again. Dare I be late, I already know not to be, so I say in a quivering voice, "Thank you."

If she thinks this is strange, she doesn't show it and just places the bag on the chair and looks at her phone. "Lucas expects you to wear the dress, word of advice, do as he says."

She half turns and I say quickly, "Excuse me."

"Yes, Miss. Quinn."

"Um, Lucas, Mr. Emiliano, um, am I safe staying here?"

I look for any sign at all that she will help me and she just nods. "If you do as he says, he will be the perfect gentleman. Word of advice, Miss. Quinn, Lucas doesn't play by the same set of rules as the rest of us. He makes them up as he goes along and expects those closest to him to make it happen.

Know one thing, I have worked for him for five years and couldn't wish for a better boss. He's not kind, you probably know that already. He's not one for polite chat and to be honest, I've never known him entertain at all. He keeps his private life to himself, so we are both in undiscovered territory here. However, know one thing, my loyalty is to him, Tom's loyalty is to him and we will never let him down. Have a nice evening, Miss. Quinn, I hope the dress fits."

I watch her leave and part of me admires her. She must know this is wrong, surely. Then again, what do I know of their world? Maybe the rules are different here. Perhaps I should just run with it, play along and then make it home with a memory of how the other half live.

My attention turns to the garment bag and I am curious to see what's inside.

At least one problem has been solved because he can't blame me for this one if it's a dog.

As I slip the dress from the bag, a note is attached and I feel my heart beat faster when I see typed instructions.

No underwear required.

What the... The blood rushes to my head as I imagine Dixie typing that. If she didn't, then she certainly read it and now what must she be thinking?

No underwear, why? I hold up the dress and gasp as the luxurious silk fabric brushes against my skin. The emerald green fabric is a perfect match for my eyes and I feel heated just imagining myself in this dress. Its soft fibers will cling to my skin leaving nothing to the imagination and I blush at the thought of him casting those deadly eyes up and down my body as I stand before him.

I almost wish I could wear the peasant dress because I would at least feel dressed in that. This is one big red flag to me because it's obvious what he wants. Just his actions earlier tell me that and yet, there's the dark part of my soul that is keen to know what that would feel like. An experience I would never get again. To be with a man like Lucas Emiliano—hell, to be *with* Lucas Emiliano, what would that feel like? Despite every part of me that says no, there's a small part of me shouting above the rest because that's the part of me I know I will listen to when the chips are down.

7 pm - destiny or downfall.

CHAPTER 9

LUCAS

*N*ow I'm in a better mood. As soon as I left my apartment, I had my head back in the game.

Just one taste of Ella was all I needed to regain control of my mind. I love the fight in her, the challenge in her words and the derision in her gaze. I love everything about her except for one thing; I haven't broken her yet.

Dixie was curious when I asked her to arrange the dress for this evening. The fact I picked it out myself from Dior and had them arrange delivery, shocked her a little. Just imagining Ella naked under the finest silk has given me a permanent hard on which was mighty uncomfortable during my meeting with Hastings Wallace, the journalist who has hounded me for months. The fact she came onto me the whole time and kept flicking her gaze to the bulge in my pants, made her think it was all for her.

Thinking about the amazing article she's sure to write just to win a dinner invitation makes me laugh inside. She's certainly attractive enough and ordinarily I would even consider a one nighter with her but not now. Not now I have Ella Quinn. My wild flower who is ripe for the picking. The innocent creature who is both appalled and fascinated by me in equal measures.

Maybe this inconvenience could be just what the doctor prescribed because I haven't felt so alive in years. This is different, interesting and completely unlike the games I usually play. Maybe I'll keep her, not tell her when the coast is clear and use her for my own distraction. She will never know unless I tell her, so as I wrap up the meeting with Hastings, Ella Quinn's fate is sealed. She's mine now until I get bored. Then she can go home safe in the knowledge it's over —but not until I say it is.

DIXIE LOOKS up as I pass her desk at 6.30. She smiles because the only time I leave this early is if I have a function to attend and she knows that's not the case this time.

"Have a good evening, Lucas."

"You too, Dixie, any plans?"

"Dinner with Johnson's parents."

I pull a face and she laughs. "My thoughts exactly."

"Then don't go."

"Difficult. We're not all like you, sir. Some of us have to do what's expected for the greater good."

"Then I pity you."

"Thank you, sir."

She grins and I nod as I walk away. Dixie is engaged to Johnson Bowdray, an up-and-coming politician who rolls with the right people at the right time. Despite not being from the right family, Johnson is besotted with my assistant after I introduced them one weekend at my ranch in the mountains. Occasionally I invite business contacts for a recreational weekend to secure my business, and this was one of them. To be fair, I like Johnson, if I didn't, he would never have been invited and having a senator in my tight circle won't be a bad thing. The organization I belong to controls rather than obeys, and it's not unusual for us to whisper words of change in an official ear. Ryder holds the same power and there are three more of us, which is why this shit needs sorting because if someone knows about the significance of the gold coin, our very organization is in jeopardy.

It takes me thirty minutes to shower and change, and tonight I plan on capturing my prey. I dress accordingly and pull on my black suit, paired with a black shirt. All in black to match my heart and the thoughts I have for passing the evening. Ella Quinn will provide a pleasing sacrifice and I will enjoy a pleasant evening doing something decadent and wrong on so many levels.

I wait for her in the dining room just before 7. Despite the heat in Vegas, I have the air conditioning turned up high and have lit a fire in the huge fireplace that dominates the room. Tom has done a good job in setting the scene and the candles that burn on every surface add to the heat and the intensity in the room.

The food is resting under the silver domes on the side and the champagne is on ice in the bucket on the stand by my seat. Everything is set for an evening of pleasure and I am impatient to play hard.

On the dot of 7 the door opens and Ella heads nervously into the room. I just stare in amazement at the change a dress can make. She looks astonishing as she tries to walk in the six-inch heels I had delivered around an hour ago, and I appreciate the effort she has made with her hair and make-up. Her dark hair is swept to the side and fastened with a beautiful emerald encrusted comb, another gift from me that I couldn't pass by. My balls tighten when she moves because the fact she's naked under the dress is evident as her nipples peak and push against the silken fabric. She looks nervous and I'm not surprised because I can be an intimidating bastard when I want to be and I want to be most of the time.

"You look beautiful, Ella, I'm happy to see the dress fits."

"It does, thank you."

She's nervous and I hand her a flute of champagne and say in a low voice, "Come and stand by the fire."

She crosses the room and takes the glass, and I see the nerves reflected in her eyes. She almost can't look at me, and I'm the bastard who loves every minute of it.

"So, you have some questions."

She's straight down to business, which impresses me. There is no lingering gaze, no apparent flirting in her eyes, and no desire to trap me in any way. Just a woman who is keen to do what she must before being set free. It's a shame she doesn't know what will that involve.

"Yes, the woman who came to collect the coin, what can you tell me about her?"

"Not a lot. She was pretty, blonde hair, I can't remember the color of her eyes though. Average height but she had a hard edge, looked as if she knew her way around town if you know what I mean."

"So, she was a whore?"

Ella blushes and says softly, "Maybe, I don't know."

"Anything else, any tattoos, defining features, jewelry?"

"Not that I can think of, except she did have a fluffy keyring, you know, the kind hotels use sometimes."

"What was it?" This piece of news interests me because if she can describe it, we may just know where she came from.

Ella's eyes narrow and she appears to be thinking hard. "It was white, a lamb I think, or it could have been a polar bear. It had black ribbon around it."

"I'll get it checked out. Anything else?"

"She seemed nervous, as if she was being followed. I

51

didn't think it strange though, a lot of my customers feel nervous, usually because they don't want to be seen buying something that's fake."

"Did you see anyone waiting outside, the car she used?"

"I think she had her own. It was pulled up outside and I remember thinking how smart it was. Almost brand new actually."

"Make, model?"

"I'm a bit rubbish at cars, they don't interest me. It was the color that struck me, nothing else."

I hide a smile. Typical woman.

I roll my eyes. "So, what color was it?"

"Electric blue with a silver stripe. I remember thinking it looked quite cool."

I make a mental note of everything she tells me because I will get this all checked out.

She seems a little more at ease, so I pull out a chair. "Take a seat, we should eat, you must be hungry."

She sits as gracefully as she can manage given the fact she obviously can't walk on the heels I gave her and the dress is obviously longer than she's used to and wraps around her legs. She almost falls into the seat and looks so mortified I want to laugh out loud. Instead, I fix her with a dark look.

"Practice your walking, if you want to go anywhere in public with me, you need to look and act as if you belong by my side."

"What if that doesn't concern me? Why would I want to be by your side, anyway, you know you're a little presumptuous, *Lucas*?"

She can't help herself and her sarcastic use of my name gives me all the ammunition I need as I fix her with a dark look and say roughly, "Are you answering me back, Ella?"

The memory of what happened earlier comes back to bite her, and she backtracks—fast.

"Of course not, I'm sorry, sure, I'll practice walking in heels, I could use learning a life skill."

She mutters something under her breath and I say angrily, "What did you say?"

"Nothing, um, just telling myself not to be such a bitch, nothing bad."

"Do you take me for a fool, Ella?"

"Um, no."

She looks worried, and the bastard in me loves every minute of this exchange.

"Then what did you say?"

She shrinks in her seat and I can tell she is trying desperately to think of another answer and mutters, "I, um, just said I'll practice walking in these heels, um, over your head."

She blushes and looks away, and I love every minute of it. Not that she will know that, because I growl.

"Stand up, Miss. Quinn, now, if you know what's good for you."

As she looks up in fear and slowly rises, it begins.

CHAPTER 10

ELLA

I've blown it. I couldn't keep my mouth shut, and he did warn me but I went there, anyway. Maybe it's because I was lulled into complacency by his easy manner and the champagne, but I forgot the one thing he told me not to do. I talked back.

Now it looks as if he's going to punish me for my audacity and my knees shake as he growls, "Come here."

My heart beats so fast I hope it gives out on me. In fact, that's not such a bad idea. Maybe I can fake an illness or something because he has a murderous look in his eyes. Trying it out for good measure, I say faintly, "I don't feel so good."

"Come here."

He repeats his sentence and I try to put one foot in front of the other and wobble precariously. It doesn't help that I'm shit scared right now, and the heat from the fire is battling my nerves and raising the temperature inside me as I slowly move toward him.

He watches me the whole time, those dead, dark eyes stripping me bare, and I watch as he devours my body with that look alone. The fact I'm naked under this dress isn't helping much because I feel so exposed as I cross the room.

The fact I'm such a klutz doesn't help either because as my heel gets caught in the hem of the dress, I am horrified to hear a ripping noise and as if in slow motion, my knees give way and I find myself heading straight for the floor. I cry out in alarm, but that's the last sound I hear as a sharp pain strikes me on the side of my head and then the world turns black.

∼

MY HEAD HURTS and I hear voices talking so loudly, it's almost as if they're shouting and I groan.

"She's coming round."

"Thank God for that."

I recognize Lucas, but the other voice is new to me and I struggle to open my eyes.

It all appears blurry and then a white light hits my eyes and I moan, snapping them shut.

"Ella, what day is it?"

"Judgment day." I groan and I swear Lucas laughs.

"Tell me what day of the week it is."

"Friday, I think."

To be honest, it could be any day of the week for all I know and the voice sounds worried. "Then where are you?"

I obviously got question one wrong, judging by the tone of his voice.

"I'm in prison."

Again, I swear I hear Lucas laugh and the other voice sounds annoyed.

"What's your name?"

"Idiot."

"She's fine doctor, can't you tell."

"I can tell nothing, she sounds delirious."

I stifle a giggle and it hurts and I wince as I touch my hand to the throbbing feeling on my head.

"Can I have an Advil please?"

"Then tell me your name."

Feeling resigned to playing the good patient, I say softly, "My name is Ella Quinn. I'm in Vegas as a guest of Lucas Emiliano, although his hosting skills leave a lot to be desired. I obviously can't walk in heels and apparently, I need to work on that, although I'm not sure why. I am now officially the clumsiest person in the world, and I'm starving. Can I have the Advil now please?"

I blink and open my eyes and almost pass out with shock because I appear to lying on the floor where I must have fallen, with my head in Lucas's lap. It feels a little awkward as he looks down at me with a mixture of concern and amusement and I close my eyes and whisper faintly, "I am so embarrassed."

The other voice speaks, making me open my eyes to put a face to it, and I see a man not much older than Lucas looking at me with concern.

"I'm Doctor Steele, Lucas called me when you fell. You hit your head on the table on your way down, you may have concussion."

"I have a headache."

The doctor smiles. "I'm sure you have. Can you stand?"

"If you take these heels off, I'll try."

The doctor nods and makes to help me and Lucas snaps, "I'll do it."

I don't miss the surprise on the doctor's face as Lucas shifts so I am sitting on his lap and growls, "Bend your leg."

"Oh, it's…"

"Goddamn it woman, bend your leg and let me remove your shoes."

The doctor shakes his head as I quickly do as he says, and just feeling Lucas's fingers against my skin makes my heart skip a beat.

He removes the shoes and my feet dance for joy and I exhale with relief. "Thank God."

"You're welcome."

Lucas grins and I can't help but giggle and for a moment it feels nice. He's taking care of me, not scaring me, and I'm surprised at how good that feels.

In one swift move, he stands with me in his arms and places me gently on the chair where I was sitting before and for some reason I'm sad about that as he straightens up and looks at me with concern.

The doctor says quickly, "She should get checked out at the hospital, she may have concussion."

Lucas looks angry and I feel like such a liability.

"Is that really necessary?" I say it quickly to try to relieve some of the tension and before he can answer, Lucas says, "Of course it's necessary. I'm taking no chances."

The doctor nods. "I'll arrange an ambulance."

"You are kidding—right?"

I stare at them in surprise and Lucas shakes his head. "No, I'm not and we'll take the helicopter."

"Now I know you're kidding."

I stare at him in total disbelief and the doctor rolls his eyes. "A little unnecessary, I mean it's only a short drive away."

"We will take the helicopter."

Lucas lifts his phone and barks instructions into it, and the doctor kneels before me and smiles. "Humor him, he's in shock just as much as you, and that man doesn't do shock well."

I'm so surprised and look across at Lucas, who snaps his phone shut.

"They're waiting for us. Do you need a ride, Luke?"

"No, I'm good and if I'm quick, I'll make dessert."

He grins and I notice he's dressed in a tux and feel sorry that we obviously interrupted his evening.

"I'll call ahead and tell them to expect you."

Turning to me, he says gently, "It's just a precaution, nothing to worry about."

As he turns to leave, I think on what he says because little does he know, I have *everything* to worry about.

CHAPTER 11

LUCAS

*A*s soon as she passed out, I was frantic, which surprised me. I don't do concern, and I'm certainly never bothered if someone passes out in front of me. But she hit her head and the fact she was out cold shocked me. I felt responsible for that so I called Luke and luckily, he was dining in the restaurant downstairs. As soon as she came round, I felt so much relief that surprised me more than the shock of her passing out in the first place.

Oddly, I want to be the one to do everything for her. I lifted her head into my lap to make her more comfortable, and I liked how that felt. I loved it when she sat on my lap and I removed her shoes. Her small giggle made me happy, and her quick wit amused me. Ella Quinn is a woman that intrigues me the more time I spend with her, and we haven't even got to the good bit yet. I like her as a person and not for what she can give me. The fact she probably despises me is inconvenient, but not insurmountable.

As I sweep her into my arms, she stiffens and says quickly, "What are you doing?"

"Carrying you to the helicopter."

"I can walk."

"No, you can't, you just demonstrated that."

"I have other shoes. I'll change, I can't go in this dress."

She looks down at the ruined dress that is tangled around her legs and the bastard in me says darkly, "You will wear what I tell you. Remember, you are my prisoner and that hasn't changed. If you speak one word out of turn, I will finish what I was about to get started."

She stiffens and I love it. She's scared, I want her to be scared, I want to get her checked out so I can check her out, preferably tonight.

As I carry her from the room toward the elevator that will take us to the roof, I'm loving the power I have over her. I'm a man who loves to take charge of every aspect of his life, and until I get her under control and under me, I won't be happy.

As soon as we step out onto the roof, she clings on tight and I can tell she's nervous. My beautiful bird is waiting to fly and as always, I feel the rush of adrenalin that gives me a greater high than any drug.

I love my toys and this is one of my favorite ones and as the pilot holds open the door, I settle Ella inside and fasten her seatbelt, making sure my fingers brush against those breasts I can't wait to experience. She shivers and as our eyes meet, I make sure mine are loaded with promise. This doesn't end tonight; it's only just beginning.

I take my seat beside her and as the bird flies, she reaches out and grasps my hand tight. I can tell she's close to hyperventilating and I lean down and say loudly, "Relax, enjoy it."

"Easy for you to say, do you really enjoy this?"

She groans as the copter dips and I laugh. "I love it."

"I always knew you were mad."

She grins alongside her words and I laugh, squeezing her hand a little tighter.

As Luke said, it doesn't take long and I note the team of medics waiting on the roof and laugh to myself. Even in a non-medical emergency, money talks and Ella will get the best care possible because I pay for it.

She is whisked away by the medical staff and I walk beside them, keeping a watchful eye over my captive.

The fact she's dressed like a million dollars doesn't register with these people because this is Vegas and they are used to it.

It doesn't take long for them to X-ray her head, check her over for any signs of concussion, and then discharge her back into my care. Once again, as I belt her in, she shivers a little and I whisper in her ear, "Are you hungry, little flower?"

Her chest heaves and she shakes her head. "I've kind of lost my appetite."

Nodding, I take my seat beside her and leave her to her own thoughts while I plan my next move. The night may have hit a temporary bump in the road, but I'm still on the journey and it ends when I say it does.

ONCE AGAIN, I carry her into the elevator and her heavy breathing tells me she's feeling the effects of being in my arms.

I remain silent and as we head into the apartment, I walk the opposite way from the dining room.

"Where are we going?" She sounds nervous and shifts a little in my arms, and I ignore her and carry on until we reach my bedroom.

She stiffens when she sees where we are and her voice shakes. "Um, why are we here, my room is the other way?"

Setting her down on the bed, I stare down at her with the dark look I wear so well. "The doctor said you couldn't be left, I need to monitor you through the night, standard procedure with a head injury."

To be honest, the doctor said shit but this suits my agenda and she can't argue with that, so she nods and then says nervously, "Thank you but this is all a little unnecessary. I'm sure I'll be fine, maybe I can call you if I feel funny."

Turning my back on her, I head to my closet and return with the only thing I could think of. "Here, you can wear this, now remove the dress."

Her eyes are wide in shock as she clutches the t-shirt I threw at her. She swings her legs to the side of the bed and makes to leave, and the bastard in me decides to play with my mouse. "Where do you think you're going?"

"To change, unless you're prepared to give a girl a little privacy."

Once again, I love the fire in her eyes as she can't help snap back and as my eyes narrow and I stare at her with an angry look, she visibly pales but stares at me defiantly.

In two steps I'm beside her and reach for her throat and her eyes widen as I tear the god damned dress from her body, relishing the sound of ripping fabric and the shock in her eyes. As I expected she is naked beneath it and as her breasts spring free I think I experience heaven and she screams and instinctively raises her arms to cover her nudity. Grabbing the t-shirt, I grip her arms with one hand and place it over her head with the other and as it falls around her body, I snarl, "Don't answer me back—ever, you won't like what I'm capable of. Now, get into bed while I fetch the meds and water. Don't move a muscle and you *will* be a good patient, or so help me God, I'll show you what happens when I'm pissed off."

She scrambles under the covers and looks at me in fear as

I turn and leave the room, feeling so turned on I can't walk straight. I'm loving every second of this power play because it amuses me to control another person. It always has and the rewards are making it so much sweeter just imagining her curled up beside me till morning.

CHAPTER 12

ELLA

I can't stop shaking. What is happening to me? First, I knock myself out because I can't do that one thing women are supposed to know instinctively - walk on heels and now I'm wearing Lucas Emiliano's shirt, tucked up in his bed, waiting for the man himself to join me.

Just thinking about what that may mean makes me feel excited and afraid in equal measures. This whole experience is turning out to be something else and just thinking back a few days when I was safe and happy in the knowledge my family were ok, seems like light years away.

I daren't move. The man's an animal and obviously has no regard for doing the right thing. Who treats another person like he does?

Lucas Emiliano, the Casino King.

The fact I'm surrounded by such luxury has not gone unnoticed. His bedroom is even bigger than the one I've been enjoying. It's absolutely immense and yet appears empty despite the luxurious furnishing and attention to every detail. This room has no life in it, it's cold and emotionless, much like its occupier and I shiver as I think of the man who rests his head here. Just thinking of the previous occupants of this bed makes me shake a little because I'm guessing a man like that is used to perfection. Supermodels, actresses perhaps, certainly not a copycat from downtown, fresh out of college.

I hear footsteps and prepare myself for another game of cat and mouse because I'm under no illusions that's what this is to him—a game and I'm the prize at the end of it. I'm not stupid, or deluded enough to think it's a game I can win, I know better than that and as he sets the glass down on the table beside the bed, he opens his palm and I see the two pills nestling in the center of it. "Take these, they will help with the pain."

"What's this, drugging me to sleep in your bed?"

I grin to take the sting from my words, although I mean them that way, he just doesn't need to know that.

He sits on the edge of the bed and it dips slightly and picks up the glass of water, holding it to my lips. His gaze is intense as he watches me pop the pills into my mouth and as the cool water slides down my throat, he nods his approval.

"Good girl."

For fuck's sake, when did I become a girl who positively glowed inside at a compliment from a bully and a bastard but that's how I feel now and I'm horrified at myself? If I was a cat, I'd be purring right now as he strokes my face and whispers, "Does it still hurt?"

I shift awkwardly. "A little."

His eyes darken and I quickly pull a face and wince—purely out of self-preservation and say, "Actually, it does throb a little."

He grins. "I know that feeling."

He laughs out loud at the horror on my face, and the fact it must be burning right now doesn't make me feel any better. I try not to look, but my eyes shift lower and I almost whimper when I see the evidence of the throbbing between his legs.

He strokes my face lightly, almost absentmindedly, and then shocks me by saying, "Tell me about yourself, why the store, it's an odd choice?"

"Not really. It's what paid my way through college. People will pay a lot of money for something bespoke."

"You don't say."

He shakes his head and I say tentatively, "The coin, what does it mean, why is it so… well, destructive?"

"It isn't. the coin is an inanimate object that just represents something. It's that I'm worried about."

He doesn't appear to be in a hurry to stop petting me like an animal and yet I quite like it, so I say hesitantly, "The woman who collected it, um, how did she die?"

"A bullet though the brain, messy business."

Thinking of his gun that is never far from his side, I wonder if he had anything to do with it and edge away a little.

"It wasn't me."

"So, you're a mind reader now?"

He laughs softly. "You're like an open book. Every thought in your head shows in your eyes."

"It doesn't."

"Are you saying I'm wrong?"

"Ok, what am I thinking now?"

I stare at him with a blank expression and he laughs. "That I'm an asshole and you can't wait to be rid of me."

"Ok, you win."

I laugh and he smiles. "That's better."

"What is?"

"Seeing you smile, it lights up your face."

"Smooth criminal."

"Is that what you think?"

"Aren't you? I mean, you carry a gun, you live in a fortress and you have more money than the federal reserves—allegedly, so how does a man your age get to be where he is today and become part of some exclusive club that thinks kidnapping young girls is ok?"

Once again, I kick myself for going too far because his eyes change in an instant and the storm enters them.

Quickly, I backtrack, "I'm sorry, disregard my earlier comment."

He relaxes a little and then, to my surprise, says abruptly, "You need to sleep. I have work to do, I'll check on you in a while."

"Um, ok."

Feeling as if I've just dodged a bullet, I watch him leave and as the door closes, I start to breathe again. He's leaving, I'm unharmed and …

Thumping the pillow in despair, I hate the fact I feel disappointed about that. Why do I want to push him, to see how far he'll go? I should be happy, pleased to be off the hook and safe and secure in the knowledge he doesn't really want me that badly. But I'm not, I want him to show me how dark light can be. How sinful it feels to explore outside the box. I want to fall into hell with him dragging me in after him because Lucas Emiliano is a paradox, a man of extremes and if this is the one time in life I get the chance to enjoy the ride, I'm in, one hundred percent.

SOMETHING FEELS STRANGE. I wake up and the room is in darkness and I'm not alone. There appears to be a body wrapped around mine. I lie stiff and afraid as that leg holds me down and a strong arm is cupping my breast as the owner breathes against my neck. This t-shirt is a fucking disgrace because it has ridden high above my waist and a man's dick is nestling between my butt and I blink rapidly in the hope I'm dreaming. What was in those pills? Surely, I would have woken when he came to bed because I'm under no illusion this is Lucas cradling me so close. Despite the horror of my situation, I'm actually feeling quite turned on right now and wonder if this is the moment I lose every last shred of my self-respect because if he makes one move in my direction, I can't be trusted not to fold on impact.

My heart hammers inside me and I think it must wake him because he stirs and I tense as his cock stiffens against my butt and his hand squeezes my breast hard.

I feel mortified that I'm as wet as Niagara Falls down below because my body appears to crave this man more than food right now and I shiver a little as I wait for his move.

His rough stubble grazes against my neck and soft lips kiss the tingling skin softly and lazily. He makes no effort to move away from my body and if anything, he presses in deeper.

Deciding I must do something for my own sanity, I pull away quickly and in doing so, something falls on the floor and I note the water pooling on the carpet beside the bed.

"Oh my god, I'm so sorry, let me clean that up?"

Strong hands pull me back to his side and he murmurs, "I'm not finished with you yet."

I stiffen in disbelief and his low chuckle rumbles against my skin.

"What are you doing?" I freeze as his hand starts caressing my thigh, and he groans, "Checking you for injuries."

"It was a fucking glass of water you moron."

I try to get away but it's useless, and he laughs. "I love it when you fight back."

"Ok, you've had your fun." My voice is slow and deliberate as if I'm talking to a person with a very low IQ. "Now, if you'll excuse me, I need to pee and clean my teeth, I mean nobody likes morning breath, especially me."

I squeal as he rolls on top of me and pins me down with his body and as he stares into my eyes, I see the amusement in his. "Relax, darlin', I'm not about to do anything about it, I just like having someone to warm my bed for once, it's different—for me, anyway."

"I doubt that, I'm not that naïve."

He grins "Well, it's the truth. You have the honor of being the first woman to do so, so congratulations, your certificates in the post."

"You mean you don't have a different woman, or even women in here every night, come on, Mr. Emiliano, do you think I was born yesterday?"

To my horror, he runs his hand down my body as if he owns it, and I hate that I love every minute of it.

"It's the truth, I fuck women in one of my suites, never my home."

I wince at his words, hating the picture he paints and I snap back, "Well, I fuck my men anywhere I can, my home, their home, the subway."

He laughs out loud. "The subway, now I know you're lying."

Leaning down, he takes one of my breasts into his mouth and bites down hard and I scream. "Ow, what the fuck was that?"

"Punishment for talking about other men."

"Why?"

"Because you're mine and you don't fuck with anyone except me."

"Now I know you're delirious. How much did you have to drink last night because number 1, I'm not yours to fuck and number 2, *we* haven't fucked and…"

"Number 3, you will shut the fuck up unless you want me to demonstrate my ownership of you right now."

I stop talking.

He rolls off and I take my chance and scoot from the bed and he says tersely, "We need to shower and eat. It's later than normal and I have meetings to attend."

"Go ahead then, don't let me stop you and call me a cab, I have a business to open."

"Nice try little flower, but you're coming too."

"I'm sorry."

He shifts from the bed and I cover my eyes when I see his cock pointing in my direction.

"I'm not letting you out of my sight."

CHAPTER 13

LUCAS

I am having so much fun right now, and I haven't even sampled the goods. Ella is an amusing play-thing. She reacts to just about every word out of my mouth with horror and indignation. Then there's the naughty part of her I love. The fact she wants me so badly she hates herself and that one move from me would get everything I want and she would hate herself almost immediately afterward. I'm loving this game and I'm keen to carry on playing it, so I point toward the bathroom. "Shower - now."

To my surprise, she quickly turns and heads that way and I'm guessing she thinks I'll wait—I won't.

As I follow her inside, she has two hands on the hem of the t-shirt and says in shock, "What are you doing?"

"Showering."

"But…"

"With you."

She looks at me in horror and I shrug. "Doctor's orders in case you pass out again. I mean, that blow to your head could affect you at any moment. I don't want you to die on me, I mean, just imagine the bad press, so this is how it must be. Sorry for the inconvenience but well, not sorry."

She stares at me open-mouthed as I reach her and finish the job she started. Hauling the t-shirt off her like it's nothing, she shrieks as I tuck her under one arm and carry her caveman style to the shower. As the warm jets spray over us from all directions, I set her down and grab the shower gel, rubbing it between my palms and soaping her body liberally. "What the..."

She is so shocked words fail her and I pay extra attention to the valley between her breasts, briefly wondering what she'd do if I put my dick there instead. Savoring the image, I spin her around and pull her tight against my body and allow my hands to roam over her skin, loving how good she feels on me.

I nip her neck gently and despite every part of her that is trying to resist, she shivers against me and a small moan escapes. My cock aches so hard as I push against her and she whispers, "That feels so good."

I allow myself a small moment of triumph as I bend my lips to graze against her neck and love the delicious tremor her body creates in mine. The steam from the shower heightens my senses and I briefly consider finishing the job right here. It wouldn't take much; I'm guessing she's ready and willing, but where's the fun in that?

So, I spin her around and say roughly, "Soap me."

Her eyes widen and I fix her with a dark look and hand her the shower gel. Squeezing it into her palm and smirking like the cocky bastard I am.

"All of it."

Her hands shake as she starts to work the gel into my body and as she reaches lower, I growl, "On your knees."

My cock is dancing like a river dancer right now as it begs for release. Her face is inches from it, and I wonder what she'd do if I told her to suck. That image is looking good right now, but she is a wicked woman because she turns the tables on me and cups my balls, saying huskily, "Stand still."

I feel her gently rolling them in her hands and resist the urge to groan out loud as she takes her time, tormenting me and seeing how far I'll go before I break.

Then she rubs the lather against my shaft, slowly, provocatively, with long hard strokes.

This is not turning out quite what I had in mind and make to pull away and she says firmly, "Don't give what you can't take. Man up and see this through."

She laughs softly as I growl, "Be careful, this beast bites."

"Then it's a good job I have sharp claws to protect myself."

She drags her nails against my shaft and I almost come on the spot. Fuck me, that feels so good and she doesn't let up because I feel her hot breath against my cock as her lips hover dangerously close. One move and she could take me inside and there is absolutely nothing I can do about that and so I become the mouse to a very sexy copycat.

I try to focus on spreadsheets, coins, even Ryder fucking King and his bunch of bastards, anything to distract me from what I want so badly right now. I refuse to let her humiliate me in my own shower, so I pull her up and push her hard against the shower wall, my hand on her throat and one hand deep between her legs. She starts to pant, more with excitement than anything, and I growl, "That's enough. I haven't forgotten I owe you one punishment, if not two, don't add a third to the list."

"Seriously."

Her eyes are wide and I smirk. "I'm always serious because I get my kicks from control, haven't you figured that out yet? Play with the devil and he ruins your soul, you have been warned. Just so you know, I play hard and I doubt you will keep up, so do as your told and spare yourself the image of me when I am seriously pissed off."

Grinding my mouth to hers, I unleash all my pent-up frustration into that kiss. I'm not careful. I'm not gentle and if her lips are bruised and swollen after this, all the better. I want to push my little flower to extremes because I'm guessing it would be worth the effort. For now, though, I will enjoy playing with her in the only way I know how. This should be quite an interesting day.

"WHAT THE FUCK ARE YOU WEARING?"

I stare at her in disbelief as she heads into the living area. After the shower, I told her to go and get dressed and I'd meet her at breakfast. Tom has pulled out all the stops this morning and as I settle on my chair by the window and grab a much-needed mug of coffee, I'm astonished when she heads inside the room wearing something Dolly Parton must have designed.

"Don't you like it?"

She spins around, giving me the full effect of a white peasant style dress, with a lace up bodice that is doing little to contain her breasts. The waist nips in tight and flares out to a skirt with more frills than a flamenco dancer's gown.

It stops just short of the knee and despite myself I am so hard just imagining unlacing that bodice and watching her tits spill free and I shake my head.

"Darlin', I love that dress, but only because I want to ruin you in it. It's certainly not suitable for what I have in mind today, so go and change."

I lift my mug and love the defiance in her eyes as she heads my way and sits down heavily on the chair. "Tough, this is all I've got except for cut-offs and a t-shirt. I have some jeans, but I'm guessing they're not appropriate either. I used to have an evening gown before some idiot ripped it to shreds, so tough luck, baby, it's the dress or nothing at all."

"Then nothing at all it is."

Her eyes widen and I resist laughing out loud at the horror on her face and growl, "Take it off."

"No."

She looks shocked and I shrug. "Do you want me to rip that one as well?"

"Fine, just tell me what I'm supposed to do then. I have no clothes because you are, 'newsflash' holding me hostage here and I didn't think to pack a designer wardrobe for my incarceration. The only thing I can wear is the skirt and top I came here in, so what's your plan?"

Lifting my phone, I punch in Dixie's number and despite the early hour, she answers immediately.

"Morning, sir."

"Morning, Dixie. I need a new wardrobe for my guest. Business, evening, day, lingerie, you know the kind of things required. Have them sent to my apartment in one hour."

"Yes, sir."

I cut the call and Ella looks at me in shock.

"One hour, that poor woman must be tearing her hair out."

"I thought I was being generous."

I jerk my thumb to the coffee.

"Help yourself, you have one hour to eat."

She is obviously hungry and doesn't need a further invitation, and as she falls on the food, it pleases me a lot. I love a woman who eats well and I love watching her groan at the light fluffy pancakes and warm pastries, not to mention the hot eggs and bacon that melt in the mouth. By the time she's finished up, she has a contented glow to her face that mesmerizes me.

"You like your food."

"Are you saying I'm GREEDY?"

She raises her eyes and I laugh softly. "You know that's not what I'm saying."

"Do I? I only know that you have insulted my fashion sense and made me feel inferior. The fact I just stuffed my face with more food than I usually eat in a month has probably shocked you more than my peasant dress."

"I wasn't shocked."

"Yeah, right."

"I was turned on."

She swallows hard and her mouth drops open as I lean across the table. "It took all my self-control not to pounce and rip that dress from your body and plunge my throbbing cock deep into the valley of your tits. I wanted to see you ride my cock like the country girl you portray and see you scream in pleasure. The fact I want to do that more than anything is a distraction I certainly don't need right now because today is all about business and it won't be great wanting to do that every hour you are with me, so you need to dress the part and keep the fucking dress for later when I am keen to revisit that image."

She blushes a deep shade of red and words fail her and that's exactly how Dixie finds her when she breezes into the room, pushing a rail of clothes with Tom behind her carrying several boxes.

I lean back and smile at my staff. "Good timing. See what you can do with this woman, I'm struggling. You have thirty minutes before we need to leave."

If they are surprised, they don't show it and Dixie smiles at Ella. "Then we don't have long. Follow me."

Ella appears lost for words as she follows them without a backward glance, leaving me to check my emails and drink even more coffee. Today should be fun.

CHAPTER 14

ELLA

*T*om and Dixie seem to be on a mission, and I have to admire their organizational skills because they have rustled up a miracle.

Tom looks at me critically as I stand before them slightly self-consciously in a slim black pencil skirt with a pale pink silk blouse, that is showing more of my cleavage than I'd like. The panty hose and kitten heels make me feel powerful, and the smart peplum jacket that matches the skirt makes me feel feminine and yet businesslike. In truth, I feel like a million dollars, which is probably what they've spent because I know quality when I see it and what's on these rails would bank-rupt a business inside of a week.

"There, you look much better."

Dixie shares a triumphant look at Tom and they high five, making me feel like some kind of project.

Clearing my throat, I look at them with confusion. "This is all lovely and everything, but what does Lucas expect me to do today? From the looks of it, I'm to take notes or something."

Dixie grins. "He hasn't told you then."

"No." I feel as if I'm the only one out of the loop as Tom laughs softly.

"You've been promoted, honey, or should I say hired. Welcome to the team."

"Excuse me?"

I stare at them in shock and Dixie grins.

"Lucas wants you to accompany him from now on, but you need a cover story. It's no secret I'm dating a Senator and my time will be tied up a little more with him going forward. Not that it will make any difference to my job with Lucas, but the people that matter don't need to know that."

"But what does that mean for me?"

I am genuinely confused, and she smiles. "We thought it would be more natural if you are considered my assistant. Someone to take up the slack when I am busy with my wedding, etc. It will look above board and no questions will be asked. I mean, obviously no one expects you to actually do anything other than play a part, but it means Lucas is happy and that's all we want, really."

Tom interrupts. "If Lucas is happy, we are happy because our job is easier. So, honey, as I said, welcome to the team and enjoy the ride."

I feel mortified as they share a knowing look and I say quickly, "But…"

There's a knock on the door and we hear a terse, "Time's up, we need to leave—now."

Dixie springs forward, thrusting a purse at me and whispers, "Take this, everything you need is inside. Enjoy your day, you'll be fine."

She almost pushes me to the door and as it opens, I see Lucas already walking toward the elevator and I almost have to run to catch up. As soon as he reaches it, he turns and I don't miss the appreciation in his eyes as he allows his glance to run the length of me and I feel like the sexiest woman alive as he growls, "I knew this was one of my better ideas."

Grabbing my wrist, he drags me inside the elevator and before the doors are even closed, he pulls me close and whispers huskily, "This is a particular fantasy of mine that I've never indulged in. Maybe today will be that day."

Pushing him away, I say crossly, "Are you going to tell me what the hell is going on because I am losing the will to live right now? Then when you've finished explaining maybe I can actually call my mom and let her know I'm ok, I'm sorry but that part is non negotiable."

"And if I allow you the call, what's in it for me?"

He grins wickedly and I stare at him angrily and open my mouth to reply but before I know it, his mouth is on mine, kissing me deeply, hungrily and with so much passion, I forget what I was about to say. Despite how I'm feeling I kiss him back because he smells amazing, looks amazing, and I have been starved of any action for what appears to be my whole life.

Maybe this isn't so bad after all because I am enjoying his attention. I'm under no illusions the game he is playing will soon get old—with him, anyway, and he'll be onto his next victim, so maybe I'll just enjoy this attention while it lasts. At least that's what I'm telling myself.

Feeling wicked, I push him back and fix him with a stern look and the amusement in his eyes makes me frown. Leaning against the wall of the elevator, he grins. "Well?"

"Mr. Emiliano. I am sure that I don't need to tell you that such behavior is inappropriate when dealing with a member of your staff. I would ask you to respect my boundaries and act accordingly."

"My staff?"

I nod. "Yes, it has been explained to me that I am your new assistant's assistant. Therefore, I consider Dixie to be my immediate boss. I am sure that I don't have to explain to you the protocol involved here and quite frankly, I find your behavior extremely offensive and well, sexist."

His eyes flash and he says evenly, "Go on."

Taking a deep breath, I say firmly, "So, as my new employer, I must ask you to act appropriately at all times. There is also the matter of my salary."

"Ah, the salary, I was waiting for this. Go on."

The elevator shudders to a stop, and I'm surprised when he reaches across and presses the door closed. "Carry on, Miss. Quinn."

"Yes, my, um, salary. You see, the fact you are keeping me here, preventing me from earning a living and going about my business will cost you—quite a lot as it happens because if you insist on hiring me as your 'assistant's, assistant' I will, I'm afraid, have to charge you accordingly."

"Name your price."

"Well..." I pretend to think hard. "Obviously, I am a business woman at the top of her game. I mean, I am in demand for my services."

"I can understand that."

He nods as if he's deep in thought and I warm to my subject.

"Well, as you know, I am paid rather well for my work and I would expect no less if I were to take a position with you. So, as you require me to on duty 24/7 and have curtailed my freedom, in such an overbearing manner may I add, I expect to be recompensed at, shall we say, a sum of $200,000 for every week you keep me here?"

I am only kidding really because who the hell pays an assistant that much money, but it's kind of funny when I use the sum I got for the coin in the argument?

"Done, Miss. Quinn."

"I'm sorry - what?"

I blink in surprise and he nods. "$200,000 dollars for you to be available to me 24/7 for as long as I require your um, services. I will have the necessary contracts drawn up for you to sign by close of business today."

"Is that right?"

I laugh softly and he nods. "Consider it done, now, we must begin, and it starts with a meeting with my second-in-command Adam Remington. Just listen and observe, maybe take a few notes and do not make any comment or engage him in conversation, do I make myself clear?"

"Yes, um, sir."

I smile and he nods. "Good, because now you are my paid employee, I will treat you as such. Very professional and above board, after all, I would hate for you to have grounds to report me to my assistant, who would unfortunately then have to report me to myself, which would make for a very awkward conversation."

He winks as he steps outside the elevator, leaving me disguising a smile. As games go, this one is shaping up to becoming one of my favorites.

CHAPTER 15

LUCAS

It feels good having Ella running after me. Dixie and Tom have done a good job, and she looks almost believable. The sight of her in that skirt and shirt made me immediately hard, and I wonder how far I can push this flirtation.

I already know that as soon as we head back to my apartment, I will take great pleasure in ripping her out of that fucksemble and making her mine in the most basic of ways.

I'm not sure when I decided that Ella Quinn was going to be my new plaything, probably the moment she stepped into the room that first day. The fact I can't keep my hands off her has surprised me. I thought I'd hate every minute of this, waiting for Ryder to give the all clear and then calling her a cab home. The fact she's in my apartment at all was a major inconvenience, but somewhere along the line, things have changed. I have turned this to my advantage and the fact I haven't got laid in so long I've forgotten; I am keen to move this game on—tonight.

She almost runs to keep up with me, and I don't miss the curious looks of the assistants who work in their cubicles as we pass. The fact I'm here among them at all is cause for concern because most of the time I hide out in my office on my own private floor, or head out to view my assets and attend business meetings. Well, today I'm about to drop an unwelcome visit at my manager's meeting that happens every Monday morning, headed up by Adam himself, and I can't wait to see their looks when we gate crash their party.

Ella is quiet behind me and I can only imagine her mind working overtime as she wonders what I'm playing at. The trouble is, I have a business that needs my constant attention —especially now because there is trouble in paradise and I want to know why. The fact someone is messing with the five kings is bad enough, but it couldn't have come at a worse time, really.

I need to rely on Ryder to get to the bottom of that mystery while I work out who is screwing around behind my back in business because I'm not liking the murmurs from the banks and the markets regarding my new venture and it's scaring off the potential investors.

As we head inside, I relish the shocked looks as I darken their doorway, and Adam looks more surprised than most as he jumps up.

"Mr. Emiliano, I wasn't expecting you."

"Relax, Adam, I'm just here to observe." I look around the room and see my managers looking nervous and I nod. "Gentlemen, please ignore the fact I'm here, I'll just sit in if I may."

Adam nods. "Of course."

He makes to offer me his chair and I say firmly, "I will sit with my assistant in the corner. This is Ella, my newest employee, she is filling in for Dixie while she concentrates on another project. Take no notice of her, pretend she's invisible, it works for me."

I feel her bristling beside me and I laugh to myself. Like I said, today is going to be fun stirring the luscious pot that is the delectable Miss. Quinn.

We take our seats on the edge and the air is laced with so much uncertainty I wonder why they're so on edge.

As Adam tries to carry on where he left off, I'm surprised when Ella rummages in her purse and pulls out a large leather-bound notebook and pen.

Setting the purse on the floor beside her, she places the notebook on her lap and proceeds to chew the end of her pen, making it hard to concentrate on anything else. She studiously ignores me and every so often she notes something down and I'm itching to see what she's written.

As meetings go, this one is duller than most and I soon tune out as they discuss weekly stats and growth charts that I studied over my breakfast this morning while Ella was being transformed like Eliza Doolittle.

After a while, she slides her notebook across and I stare down in surprise at the words on the page.

When do I get my phone call? I was thinking right after this meeting that is incidentally the worst thing I have ever had the misfortune to sit through in my life.

Taking my pen out of my pocket, I write.

The phone call is assured as soon as we finish up here, but only if you study these people and tell me one observation about each of them.

I slide it back and she chews her pen again and looks around the room.

After about ten minutes, the notebook is back and I look at the words with interest.

The guy in the red tie, definite sleazebag. Can't stop looking down my top and doesn't think I know.

The guy to his right hasn't a clue what Adam is talking about because his mind's not in the room. He seems nervous, and the sweat on his brow makes me surmise he's nervous as hell.

The man next to Adam on the other side is a cock sucking ass licker. He nods at everything Adam says and looks around the room as if it was his idea. He couldn't be more obvious if he tried, and the rest of the room hates him. I'm guessing he's after a promotion— watch him. The last one remaining is writing everything down, and yet I'm not sure he's really listening. He keeps on looking at his Apple watch, and it's not the time that interests him. He's obviously in two meetings right now, and I'm not sure if it's business, or arranging his social life. Hopefully for him the latter because it would make me think more of him if that was the case.

Her observations impress me and I write.

One phone call earned. Well done Miss. Quinn.

As an afterthought I write, **And Adam, what do you think about him?**

I find myself more than interested in what she makes of him because she doesn't know how close we are and I almost hope she slates him because I can wind him up about that forever more.

It feels like ages before she slides the notebook back and I stare at her words in surprise. *Watch him.*

I look up and see a man doing nothing different to what he usually does and I write, **Why?**

Because he is saying what he thinks you want to hear. He keeps on looking at you as if to remind himself you're here, making me wonder if he would be saying something different if you weren't. It's all a little fake if I'm honest. They are all like coiled springs waiting to unravel if pushed and I'm guessing they only tell you what they want you to hear. I would in their position, it's human nature.

Leaning back, I think on her words and study my team a little more carefully. I've never had any reason to doubt them before, and yet there's something in her words that is ringing true. How well do I really know my employees, my friend even? I am usually hidden away in my ivory tower and, as she said, only hear what they want me to hear. I thought things were set up, a well-oiled machine that runs despite me. Maybe that's where my problems lie. I've relinquished control of my business to my managers, and maybe they are just telling me what I expect to hear and not what I need to know.

Deciding to delve a little deeper, I catch Adam's eye and hold up my hand. He stops talking and all eyes swing toward me nervously.

"I'm sorry to interrupt gentlemen, but now I have you all together, I want to ask a question."

You could cut the atmosphere in the room with a butter knife and I take my time, loving the awkward silence and the fear in their eyes. Why are they afraid, what are they hiding? That is something I need to know, so I stand and start pacing the room, a tactic that always sets people on edge and gives them nowhere to hide. Glaring at Nathan, the guy in the red tie, I snap, "I want a full report on my desk by close of business on the Cobalt project. Why are they stalling on a completion date and what's holding things up?"

I turn to Bill Bailey, my business manager who is obviously attached to his watch and snarl, "If you paid as much attention to your job as your fucking watch, I may not be fending off questions from shareholders and fielding calls from organizations who doubt we can deliver."

He appears to shrink in his seat and I snarl, "Same for you. A full report on what's holding us up and a list of shareholders who are dragging their heels. There is no reason for anyone to be getting cold feet on this project, and I want to know who's spreading doubt."

Turning to Mike who is licking Adam's ass, I bark, "Stop playing the fucking yes man and grow some balls. If I see you suck up to Adam's ass one more time, I'll shove you so deep inside it you'll pay rent. Now, do what we pay you for and do your risk assessment because if there are any obstacles in our way going forward, I'm using your head to batter them down."

Fixing my attention on the guy who appears nervous as hell, I say ominously, "What's your problem?"

He looks as if he's about to pass out as he swallows hard. "I'm sorry, sir, I don't have a problem."

"Then why are you sweating like a pig, is there something you want to share with us, or are you so far out of your depth you're struggling to breathe?"

I catch Adam's eyes and he looks more interested than anything and Brad stutters, "I'm sorry, sir, it's just..."

"Just what?"

"My, um, wife is in labor and I'm, well, worried."

I stare at him in disbelief and yell, "Well, what the fuck are you doing here, go?"

He looks up in shock and I shake my head. "Just go, why didn't you tell Adam?"

"I thought..."

"What, that we wouldn't care, that we value business over family, that we are fucking monsters? Get the fuck out of here and apologize to your wife for being such a fucking weak-willed moron, and I don't want to see you back here for one week. Work remotely and enjoy your family and if that kid isn't named after me, I will want to know why."

"It's a girl, sir." Brad smiles and just like that the worry disappears from his eyes and I smile. "Then name her Ella after Miss. Quinn. Now fuck off."

He looks so relieved I feel quite good about something for a change and as soon as he leaves the room, I growl, "Did anyone know about this?"

There's an awkward silence and Adam says sharply, "Well, did anyone know?"

Mike's voice shakes a little as he says, "He did mention something about it this morning."

Adam stares at him disbelief, "Then why did he come in?"

"Because he was worried you would fire him and with a new baby, he can't afford to be out of a job."

I hear Ella gasp behind me and feel her disapproval hit me square in the jaw from across the room.

Adam shakes his head. "Why would he think that, we're not monsters?"

I feel all eyes turn to me and know it's probably down to me. I'm such a bastard I demand full commitment from my staff and never consider they have a life outside the office. Adam himself has a new wife and yet he sees more of me than her and for a moment I feel bad about that. Then again, business is business and we are facing a shit storm approaching, so I snarl, "For the record, if your mind is not one hundred percent on the job, you are fucking useless to me, anyway. Sort your shit out before you come to work and if you need time to do that, tell Adam. Brad may as well as been the paint on the walls for all the use he was today and when he returns, he'll be way more efficient because of it. Business isn't just about physically being here, it's also about what you do when you are. So, man up, grow some balls and take responsibility for your shit and I don't expect to have to second guess every minute of your day. Now, fuck off the lot of you, I want a word with Adam—in private."

They don't need to be told a second time and as they gather their stuff, Ella jumps up and I bark, "Miss. Quinn, go and arrange some coffee. Ask one of the assistants outside to show you where to go."

She nods and looks relieved to be given a hall pass, but just before she leaves, I growl, "Oh, and Miss. Quinn..."

She turns and I hold out my phone.

"You'll need this for the call I asked you to make. Don't be long."

She looks at me in surprise and the smile on her face makes my world stop spinning. She looks so beautiful I almost stop breathing as her eyes sparkle with tears and her chest heaves with emotion. As her fingers close around the phone and brush against mine, she whispers, "Thank you."

Then she turns and leaves, and I resist every part of me that wants to race after her and pull her close and keep her there forever.

CHAPTER 16

I am glad to be out of that room. It was so intense, and Lucas obviously makes his employees nervous. I can relate to that because he is quite intimidating when he wants to be. There's a darkness to him that he keeps wrapped around himself like a shield against the world.

I'm not surprised the man was scared to take a day off and I wonder if that's true for most of them. Thinking of Tom and Dixie and how quickly they run to his side, makes me wonder what he's like when he loses his temper. They appear to bend over backwards to make him happy, and there's a part of me that wants to see that side of him.

"Excuse me, Miss. Quinn."

I stop and look behind me at the man with the red tie who was checking me out during the meeting, and my skin crawls.

"May I help you?"

I keep my tone firm and business-like and he smiles, the edges of his eyes crinkling up in the corner as he checks out my cleavage.

"I just wanted to welcome you to the family and if you

need anything come and find me because it's good to have a friend in high places around here."

He hands me his business card and as I take it, his fingers brush against mine and I snatch my hand back quickly.

"Thank you, you are very kind."

He smiles, but it makes me feel on edge as he says creepily, "Let me show you where to get the coffee, I could use one myself, after all, it looks as if I'll be here for some time. Maybe when you've finished, you'd like to meet me and grab some food after work."

"Oh, um…"

He puts his hand on the small of my back and pushes me along and whispers, "I insist, Miss. Quinn, after all, it pays to have friends rather than enemies, wouldn't you agree?"

It takes all my self-control not to stamp on his foot and punch him, but instead I allow him to propel me along and grind my teeth as he says flirtatiously. "I was surprised to see you with Lucas instead of Dixie. She's always been so firmly glued to his side the talk is they share everything, if you know what I mean. You know, if he ever behaves inappropriately, don't feel as if you can't speak out, I'm a good listener."

I am actually stunned to be having this conversation at all and wonder about Nathan. I hope he's better at his job than his dubious chat up lines and I say icily, "Sir, I'm afraid I don't know what you are talking about. If you are implying that I am incapable of dealing with an employer who over-steps the mark, you are wrong. I would also ask that you keep from touching me and only talk to me about things to do with the business. Implying that my employer is having an inappropriate relationship with the woman who is training me, is both disloyal and unprofessional, so don't let me keep you from the work I know you have waiting and don't expect me to show up later, I have other arrangements."

I turn to leave and my heart thumps as I wonder if I've

gone too far. That man deserved every word, but I must remember where I am and that this is a game I don't usually play.

Luckily, he just heads off back to his office and I swallow my nerves. Is this what women can expect in this place? Advances from the men in authority putting pressure on them to keep them happy, or else. This is so cliched it makes my blood boil, and I'm surprised when I hear a low chuckle beside me.

Spinning around, I see an older woman looking at me with interest and she holds out her hand. "Hey, I'm Carla, I work for Mr. Stevenson, the guy in charge of hospitality. I'm sorry, but I overheard your conversation and just wanted to slap you on the back and welcome you properly."

Her eyes flash with amusement and I relax. "Thanks, Carla, I'm Ella, pleased to meet you."

She nods. "Same. So, let me show you where to pick up that coffee, that is where you're heading, right?"

"Yes, thanks."

As we walk, she says with interest. "So, word is you've replaced Dixie for a bit. I'm impressed, I didn't know there was even an opening."

"No, it came as quite a shock to me too."

I laugh softly and she says with interest. "So, where are you from? You must be good to act as Dixie's replacement."

"To be honest, Carla," I lower my voice and she leans in.

"It's just a favor to Dixie. We're friends and she needed someone to fill in for her. I doubt I'll be here long, but the money's good."

I laugh to myself as she nods. "Yes, they do pay well. So, what do you usually do?"

"Oh, you know, this and that. Admin mainly, a little bit of hands-on creation too, you know art, crafts, etc."

"Well, honey, you never know, this job may open a few

doors for you. It's unusual to start at the top, but maybe when Dixie is back full time, they'll find you another slot somewhere else."

"As long as it's not with that creep, is he usually like that?"

She groans. "Nathan is well known around here. He's had more interns than the rest of the corporation put together. A serial offender when it comes to bedding his assistants and the fact his wife is the sweetest woman I've ever met, makes everyone hate him even more."

"Poor woman."

"Well, poor in every other way than money. The guys on the management floor are seriously loaded. Money makes money after all and the gambling world attracts a ton of it."

We reach the kitchen and she sets about showing me where to get everything I need and as I wait for the kettle, she sighs. "Well, I should go, I have a deadline and it's not worth getting in Jackson's bad books."

"Jackson?"

"My manager. He's nice enough most of the time, but if I fall behind, or do something wrong, he chews my ass off in front of the entire floor. Fucking bastard, then again, most of the time he's away from the office so I get my space."

She turns before she leaves and smiles. "Welcome to the Casino King's empire, honey, just don't let them ruin you."

As she leaves, I wonder about the people who work here. Just imagining a world where I was scared of upsetting anyone on a daily basis doesn't seem worth it to me. Just thinking of my own business where I don't report to anyone but me, makes me feel luckier than the lot of them put together. I may not have as much money, but is that really important? Yes, it buys you fancy clothes, nice houses and gourmet meals, but does it buy you happiness? I'm not so sure.

Remembering my phone call, I decide to take it now

before Lucas changes his mind and as I dial the familiar number, I'm surprised to see it flash up on Lucas's screen, under 'Ella's mom.' My heart beats a little faster because why would he have my mom's number programed into his phone? It doesn't make sense, but I shrug it off as soon as she answers in the soft, rather nervous voice she always uses. *"Caitlyn Quinn."*

"Mom, it's me."

"Ella, but this isn't your number, what's happened?"

"Relax mom, I, um, lost my phone and borrowed a friend's."

I hate lying to her but I there is some truth in it because I don't actually know where my phone is right now.

"Oh, Ella, I was so worried when you didn't call, are you ok?"

"I'm fine. The flight was good and to be honest, I was a little tired and slept rather a long time. Anyway, how are things in Sunny Vale, are they treating you well?"

I hear the anxiety in my voice because I'm so worried about her. She's the important part of me and just thinking of her so far away is like a serrated knife to my heart every time I hear her voice.

"It's amazing, honey, I love it. The people are so nice and helped me make my room homey and comfortable. I miss you though,"

She laughs softly. *"I missed you as soon as the door closed behind you. I wish..."*

"Don't mom." The tears burn because I know what she wants more than anything. It was always her dream to have a little house by the sea with an annex for her and me and Hannah living next door. The family together living our best life, but how is that even possible? Mom needs medical help, and Hannah is not far behind her. I need to work to pay for things and anyway, Hannah may well marry and have a family of her own. Mom's dream is just that, a dream that will never come true. Something fanciful that is not practical and is never going to happen.

She says happily, *"I spoke to Hannah yesterday, she seems to be doing well."*

"That's good to hear."

Once again, I feel bad for not checking on my sister, then mom says brightly, *"Evan was there, he's such a nice man, I wish you would find someone like him."*

"Me too, mom." Thinking of Evan makes me want to laugh. The last thing I want is to find someone like him. He may be nice enough, steady, dependable and predictable. For Hannah that's perfect, those are the qualities she values, but it never was for me. I love a bit of shade in my life, and that's why I'm probably enjoying this freak show a little more than I should. It's exciting, dangerous and shocking, and I'm loving every minute of it. Just thinking of settling down with the likes of Evan makes me bored already and mom says lightly, *"I asked Hannah if she could set you up with one of Evan's friends. You know, a blind date. She said she'd see what she could do."*

"Mom!"

I almost yell down the phone and she laughs, *"Leave it with me, honey, mommy knows best and I'll have you settled in the blink of an eye."*

"No need, I've um, found someone."

"I knew it."

I hear the triumph in her voice as she says excitedly, "Tell me about him."

"He's ok I guess, a bit moody, you know the type. Thinks he can get everything his way and expects it. I'm not sure what I think of him really, I mean, I've had better."

I laugh to myself, picturing Lucas's face if he could hear me now.

"He doesn't sound that nice, honey. Maybe we should still ask Evan."

"It's fine, I'll slap him in line, you know, mold him to my idea of greatness."

Mom laughs. *"If anyone can, you can, honey. You always were good at copying and I've no doubt at all that you have an idea of how to copy your image of the perfect man and make it happen."*

I hear voices and she says quickly, *"Sorry, I have to go, I have an appointment with the hairdresser. I'm thinking about going blonde, do you think it will suit me?"*

"Undoubtedly, everything suits you."

I feel warm inside as I hear the happiness in her voice, making me glad I went through with the job. It may have landed me in the most trouble I've ever been in, but it was worth all of this to hear mom sounding so happy.

"Talk soon, Ella, I love you."

"I love you too, mom."

As I cut the call, I feel five hundred times better. Thank goodness we spoke. It gives me strength to cope through the next few days. Although, I could leave at any time if Lucas finds answers to his questions about the coin.

I don't like the way I feel destroyed by that thought. Surely, I want to leave; return home and carry on with my business and leave this shady world behind me. Then again, since being here, I've felt more alive than I've ever done before.

Quickly, I dial Hannah's number but it cuts straight to voicemail. Just hearing her sing song voice on the recording is enough to make me smile and as I leave a message promising to call her as soon as I can, I hang up feeling heaps better than I did before. I know Hannah is ok because I would have known by the tone of mom's voice if something was up. She's probably with Evan, it is late at home, anyway.

I'm just glad they're ok because now it's time to concentrate on me. Will I be ok? I'm not so sure but I'll have fun along the way and if I'm sure of anything, it's that at least.

CHAPTER 17

LUCAS

*A*dam looks at me with a hard expression. "What's going on?"

"What do you mean?"

"The meeting, the girl - who is she by the way?"

"Ella?"

I grin, enjoying keeping something from him he is obviously itching to know about.

"Yes, Ella, where's Dixie and why wasn't I told you had a new assistant, unless…"

He laughs softly. "You bastard."

"I don't know what you're talking about."

"Don't you?" He laughs. "If I'm guessing correctly, that girl is no more your assistant than I'm your whore. Maybe I got that the wrong way round. What's this, bring a pet to work day?"

I feel unreasonably angered by his tone and snap. "Well, she *is* my assistant, and I'd thank you to keep your dirty mind focused on business."

He looks surprised. "I'm sorry, Lucas, I thought…"

"You thought shit. Now, what the fuck was that meeting all about?"

"You know what it was, the usual brainstorming of figures on a Monday morning. Why, what did you see?"

"I saw a bunch of kissassers struggling to keep their nerves in check. I saw you having a conversation but a different one going on underneath."

"What are you talking about?"

If anything, Adam looks astonished, which settles my nerves a little and I lean back.

"Nathan couldn't keep his eyes off Ella's tits, Bill was more interested in his fucking watch and Mike was so far up your ass he stunk. What's really going on, is there something I should know?"

Adam, to his credit, just sighs heavily. "You're right, I thought as much myself. Brad was obviously worrying about his wife. That checks out at least."

"Does it?"

He raises his eyes and I say slowly, "Check his story, in fact, check his records, talk to his staff and find out what he keeps locked inside his desk. Carry out a clean sweep of his office and report back. If he has any secrets, I want to know about them."

"Do you really think…"

"Yes, now, Bill. Do the same for him, send him on a trip for a few days. Silver city would be your best bet. We need to move that business on and he will be the best man to spot any weakness, if he has his full attention on business that is."

"Ok, and Nathan?"

"I don't trust him, period. Word is he screws anything with legs and a skirt. Find out the story there because I'm guessing we're one fuck away from a lawsuit. We can't risk any more bad press, so head that one off at the pass."

"And Mike?"

"Take him down a peg or two. Make him work harder for approval because he's getting too comfortable."

"Jealous?" Adam laughs.

"Of you, don't make me laugh. He can fuck your ass for all I care, I just don't like the guy. People like that climb up the ladder by sucking up rather than actual hard work. Make him earn my respect. He has a long way to go before he does."

"Anyway." I stretch out and briefly wonder how long it takes to make a cup of fucking coffee. I feel strangely irritated that Ella isn't here beside me, and I wonder about that. I miss her already, which surprises me. It must be because I haven't fucked her yet. Maybe that's all I need and yet, there's something else. Something about the way I jumped to her defense when Adam insinuated she's a whore. I also hated the fact Nathan couldn't tear his eyes from her tits and loved the way she assessed my team so easily.

Adam interrupts my thoughts of Ella and says brightly, "Penelope said she hasn't seen you much lately."

"That doesn't concern me."

He laughs. "You know what women are like. She thinks she needs to wine and dine you as my boss, keep you in a close circle so it assures our position at the top of the social elite."

"You married one of those, I'm surprised, Adam, I didn't know Penelope was like that?"

I don't miss the flicker of distaste that passes across his face as he sighs. "Neither did I?"

"Then what changed?"

He shrugs. "I'm not sure, really. Maybe I spend too long here, but she's developed a circle of friends I'm not enamored of. You know the type, socialite, gold digger, bored housewife and money grabber. Suddenly, Penelope is listening to them and accepting invitations to brunch and social drinks parties. The usual high rollers who suck up to my ass in the hope of gaining favor with you."

"Me?"

Adam laughs slightly bitterly, which surprises me.

"It's always you, Lucas. They all want to get close, push the monkey aside to reach the organ grinder. The Casino King, the man with gambling in his hand. The top dog and the prize for men and women alike. Penelope has tried to arrange dates for most of her single friends, but I've made your excuses. Told her you were busy and had your back. The trouble is, the knives, or should I say nails, are sharpening as we speak and she won't let up. It's why I prefer to be here because when I get home, she's on me like a rash and not in the way I want either."

He looks so subdued I'm shocked. He's a newlywed for Christ's sake, this is not looking good for his future.

"Tell her I'll come, arrange it."

My words take him by surprise and he looks up in shock.

"Tell her what?"

"That I'll come to her little gathering, drinks party, or whatever the fuck she's got planned, but I'm bringing a guest."

Adam laughs. "Miss. Quinn, perhaps. I knew it."

I can't help but laugh. "She'll do for the occasion. Yes, let's play Penelope at her own game and use the delightful Miss Quinn to make my point. Then she may get off your case and go back to being the horny wife you need, rather than the manipulating one."

"I can but hope." Adam shakes his head, and I feel concerned for my friend. I know it was a quick marriage, then again, we live in Vegas, it's not uncommon but part of me wonders if this was something else. Maybe Penelope had a hidden agenda that is being put in place. I hope I'm wrong but I need to know and the fact Ella will be by my side makes a dull evening more interesting.

As the door opens, I look up and see the woman herself balancing a tray as she heads inside and I can tell she's happier. The sparkle in her eyes tells me that and as she sets the tray on the boardroom table, she smiles at Adam warmly.

"I hope you like coffee. I wasn't sure if you'd prefer tea, but I brought a selection just in case."

She smiles at him so sweetly I'm instantly annoyed and just hearing her direct that soft, husky voice in his direction makes me jealous which surprises me. I don't get jealous —ever.

She turns and hands me my phone. "I'm sorry, sir, I took a few calls for you. Your doctor called and said he had that treatment for your, um, man parts ready. I told him we would swing past the clinic later. Also, Dixie called and told me the woman has left your apartment but you may need new sheets, oh and a fresh supply of condoms."

She grins impishly and I catch Adam trying to stifle a laugh.

"Anything else."

My voice is even, but I am imagining all sorts of punishments for the desirable woman who is begging for it right now as she shrugs. "No, unless the call from your lawyer can wait. He was just checking on the paternity suit concerning the lady boy from Paris who claims to be your son. Other than that, here's your coffee, sir, will there be anything else?"

"You may sit, Miss. Quinn, and if I have any further use of you, be sure I will let you know. The corner - now."

I point to the chair against the wall and laugh to myself as she nods. "Thank you, sir."

Adam starts droning on about spreadsheets again and I am so distracted because Ella takes it upon herself to cross her legs, her skirt rising high above her thighs as she chews her pen and throws suggestive looks my way. I know what she's doing and I love every minute of it because I'm under no illusion this is just a game to her. She doesn't really want me; she just wants to mess with me and I'm loving it.

Ten minutes is all I can stand before I say abruptly, "We'll leave it there. Make sure those reports are with me by 7 and organize the investigation I requested. Text me the time and place Penelope arranges; we'll leave you to it."

"No problem."

We stand and I say roughly, "Miss. Quinn, stop daydreaming and pay attention. I'm taking you on a tour so you see how things work and I don't expect you to stop concentrating for a second or I'll re-think your position in my company."

Adam rolls his eyes, but Ella just nods respectfully. "Of course, sir, I'm keen to learn. You know, I always wanted to be a croupier, I think it has something to do with watching men sweat when they stand to lose everything, such a delightful image, wouldn't you say?"

Adam laughs out loud and I storm from the room, my hand itching in anticipation of a delightful evening ahead.

Keep going, Miss. Quinn, every word has consequences and yours are about to come back and bite you.

CHAPTER 18

ELLA

I have no smart remarks left. In fact, I have no words at all because I am stunned into silence. Walking around the most expensive resort in Vegas is an eye opener of the most decadent kind. It's like walking beside royalty - the king because everyone it seems bows down before him. The further we go, the quieter I get because it's so overwhelming. The sheer scale of this enterprise has rendered me speechless, and I am so intimidated right now —by him.

We walk through the vast space and it feels as if just about everyone watches us. Lucas is obviously proud of his business as he points out little details here and there and I say slightly reverently, "This is impressive, Lucas, you must be very proud."

I stare at him in awe and he nods. "I am. In just this resort we have 350,000 feet of gambling space that contain 380 gaming tables, 6300 slot machines, and a bingo hall that can accommodate up to 5000 players."

I stare around me at an explosion of stone animals, twisting metal art, glittering chandeliers and decadent furnishings and he says with obvious pride. "Games include poker, blackjack, roulette, craps and baccarat, and there's a private room where the more affluent customers can stake large sums of money and play high-stakes games in relative privacy. For beginners, there's an excellent gaming school with lessons on technique and, just as importantly, casino etiquette. Alongside the casino, the resort offers a water park for the kids, shows, 38 restaurants and trips to the Grand Canyon by helicopter if you prefer."

"It's so vast, so amazing, I never knew."

I say in disbelief, "I never knew it was, well, fantastic."

He stares at me in surprise. "But you live in Vegas, surely you were curious, are you seriously telling me you have never been here before?"

"No, I haven't because I don't have money to waste, you know. You're right, I do live here and know how these things operate and only a fool would venture inside your domain and expect to leave richer for it."

I feel my disapproval radiating off me and Lucas laughs. "This is nothing, I have bigger, better, more luxurious resorts spreading the whole of the country, the world even. Maybe I'll take you on a tour of them. It may reverse your opinion of gambling."

"I doubt that, anyway, I have a business to run, haven't you forgotten that, not everyone has the luxury of time?"

"You think I have the luxury of time?" He laughs softly. "I have the luxury of life, money and everything that goes with it. What I am poorer for is time. Every waking hour is planned, filled with meetings, events, social engagements and business meetings. Not one hour of my day is mine to enjoy until the door closes behind me in my apartment of an evening. If I'm traveling, it's much the same. No vacation is without business attached and so you, my dear Ella, are richer than me where it counts."

His words make me feel sad and instinctively I move a little closer to him, itching to grab his hand and show him how sorry I am, then a woman stops before us and I feel him tense up as she drawls, "Lucas, you've been avoiding me."

She turns her attention to me and looks me up and down and curls her lip. "What's that?"

I shrink under her malicious gaze because this woman is well out of my league. Polished perfection with nothing left to chance. Her blonde hair is swept high on her head and looks effortlessly chic. Her make-up is a perfect work of art, and her red painted lips turn up in a smile as she bats her eyelashes at Lucas. She reaches out and drags a polished fingernail down his chest that has me clenching my fist with a mixture of shame and anger and she whispers, "I've missed you."

"Sarah." Lucas nods and then turns to me and says roughly, "Ella, meet Sarah, the biggest bitch in Vegas."

My mouth drops open at the same time as hers as he snarls, "I'm surprised security let you in after that stunt you pulled last time you were here. I'm guessing the governor didn't press charges after you tried to blackmail him for hundreds of thousands of dollars. To be honest, I was a little surprised he went for you at all after I warned him off. Then again, you've always made it easy for men who want a mean-ingless fuck with a dirty whore."

She blinks in surprise and I hold my breath as he pulls me past and nods to a man I never even saw walking behind us. As another man takes his place, I watch the previous one take her arm and whisper something in her ear. Lucas carries on walking, but I can tell he's angry and I whisper, "What was that all about?"

"Sarah Merton, high-class prostitute who thinks she can operate in my casino and blackmail my guests. She made a big mistake last time she was here and tried to blackmail a governor who was here for the weekend. It's not uncommon for them to request company, and she used to be discreet. The trouble is, she got greedy and now I won't have her anywhere near my business. If anything, I'm angry she was allowed in at all."

Suddenly, he stops and turns to face me and I see the dark storm building in his eyes. To my surprise, he reaches out and holds the palm of his hands to my face and just stares into my eyes. It feels awkward as fuck because people are staring and then he leans down and whispers, "I hated how she looked at you. Nobody will ever get away with looking, or talking to you like that when I'm around."

He seems genuinely upset and I shrug, "It's fine, I've had worse."

"Not when you're with me, you deserve respect and I will not have anyone treat you differently."

Thinking it best to keep the whole Nathan conversation to myself, I just laugh self-consciously, "Anyway, you were saying before we were so rudely interrupted."

He seems to breathe a little easier and smiles. "As I was saying, I have bigger, better, more luxurious resorts than this one. We should take that trip, let me convert you, let me corrupt your soul and drag you over to the dark side."

Feeling a delicious shiver pass through my body, I say huskily, "Are you trying to ruin me, Lucas Emiliano?"

"Miss. Quinn, if I want to ruin you, you will love every second of it and crave more. This life is a drug, it's hard, unyielding and addictive."

"I'm not talking about this life, Lucas, it's the man who fascinates me."

For a moment, he just stares and something shifts between us. I see the desire heavy in his eyes as he gazes at me long and hard. It makes me hitch my breath as I see the desire mixed with yearning and the passion he can't contain.

All around us is the sound of slot machines, talking, laughing and music. The noise tells us there is life going on, but I think both of ours stop for a moment of realization.

I feel the wind changing direction and I struggle to breathe. Lucas is battling with something; I can tell and then without another word, he reaches out and takes my hand and pulls me along with him.

"Come. There's somewhere I need to show you."

My heart pounds so fast I can almost hear it over the noise, and as I follow him to yet another elevator, I am surprised when he takes a key from his pocket and grins wickedly. "Prepare for the unexpected, Miss. Quinn. It's time to show you who you're really dealing with."

CHAPTER 19

LUCAS

I can't believe I'm really doing this. I never bring anyone here. Even most of my staff don't know about this secret part of the resort, and yet here I am, taking a relative stranger into my decadent paradise.

As we step outside the elevator, Ella gasps beside me and I stare with a huge ball of pride tearing me up inside as I look at my sanctuary. The place I come to escape the madness of Vegas and enjoy a moment of pleasure.

"Lucas, this place, it's amazing."

She stares at the mosaic covered courtyard that is edged in gold. The sun beats down on a secluded area where fountains dance in the sunlight and reflect the gold touches that are both decadent and delirious. There is no sound here at all. Just that of the exotic birds that call this their home and the intoxicating scent of the rare blooms that I had shipped in from around the world. This is my palace and I am it's king. My retreat, my sanctuary, the place I regroup and settle my spirit.

This is the only place I feel truly happy in and as I see

Ella's eyes shine with unshed tears, I know she is feeling the effects as deeply as I do.

"This is so beautiful, perfect, I never knew."

We could be in a tropical paradise right now, and I take her hand and love the shiver that passes through my body as she grips it tightly.

"Lucas, this place, it's like paradise." She sighs as we wander through the garden and her head turns in every direction as she takes in every detail of a place that drips opulence and beauty. We near a large lake that is man made but looks as natural as any of nature's miracles. The water sparkles in the sunlight and I say impulsively, "Come on, let's cool off."

"Seriously." Her eyes are wide as I make short work of my clothes and she looks around her nervously.

"It's fine." I laugh softly. "Nobody comes here. I have the key and the elevator is locked. You are perfectly safe—for now, anyway."

She giggles, and it sends a message straight to my already rigid cock and she licks her lips as I stand before her dressed in nothing but wicked intent and shyly, she slowly removes her clothes, blushing a little as I openly stare.

As soon as I see her in all her naked glory, I feel a rush of desire controlling every part of me and before I can stop myself, I pull her roughly against me and kiss her as if I need the air she breathes to survive. Her low moan sends me over the edge and every part of the decadent evening I had planned goes out of the window as my decision is made. She's mine and it's time to claim ownership.

She trembles against me, and I love how she feels. So soft, smooth and delicate, like one of my most beautiful flowers. But Ella is a wild one, untouched and natural in her beauty, and that is the best type of flower to pick. She moans against my mouth as I run my hands down her body and love how smooth she feels. Her tits graze against my chest and as my finger dips between her legs, I feel the desire sticky and sweet. Her gasp of pleasure makes me bold, and I curl a finger inside her and love how she shivers against me. Biting her neck, her gasps of pain mixed with pleasure makes me rampant and I lift one of her legs against my waist and my cock twitches at her opening. "Do you want me, Ella Quinn?"

I whisper the dark words as she moans in my arms and gasps, "Yes, I want you."

Feeling so powerful right now, I lower her leg and begin kissing a trail down her body until I kneel before her. As I part her lips and taste the honey, she shivers on my tongue and I say huskily, "Nobody can hear your screams in here, show me how much you want me."

"Please, Lucas, god, I want you so much right now."

I smile against her soft lips and love how good she tastes. This is so different to anything I've ever had, it's like a delicious game that has changed direction like a feather on the gust of wind. Suddenly, sex has meaning because I love hearing her gasps of pleasure and moans of desire. I want to please her, hear her call my name and love what I can give her.

Reaching back, I find my pants and pull a condom from the pocket. As Ella trembles against me, I sheaf my cock and then pull her gently down to sit on me. Grabbing her face in my hands, I stare into her eyes and say darkly, "Look at me."

Her eye lashes flutter open and I love the desire that changes the color to a dark smoky gray and I shift her a little so she is poised against my cock.

"I want to be inside you, Ella, is that ok with you?"

I need to ask permission for something I usually take with no consequence. It means everything to me to hear her beg, and she nods, "I want you, Lucas, I want the whole of you."

111

"I own you, Ella, you're mine, remember that."

I don't know when I got so needy because it's important to me she stays. I don't want to think of her leaving because I am getting used to her by my side. Life is way more interesting with Ella in it and I love how she bites her lip and groans, "I'm yours, now for fuck's sake put me out of my misery you bastard."

I capture her words against my lips and bite that lip that teases me and as she cries out with pain, I hold her face in my hands and say roughly, "Look at me, watch me own you."

She gasps as I pull her down onto my rock-hard cock and as I slide into a piece of heaven, I love the lust that sparkles in her eyes.

Feeling myself inside Ella is like the most expensive drug. I'm not prepared for the effects of her, and I groan as my cock dances inside her heavenly walls. She screams in pleasure and I move slowly and carefully, savoring every minute I am inside her and it feels so good I never want to leave. Her walls scrape against my hard cock and her clit drags against my shaft as I push harder, deeper, faster.

Spinning her around, I push in deeper as she lies beneath me, and I love seeing her hair spill from the binding that held it back. Her chest heaves and her legs wrap around my waist as I plunder her most private place and then she shocks me by holding her hand flat against my cheek and stares deep into my eyes and whispers, "I love feeling you inside me, it feels like home."

The wet tears on her lashes are tears of joy as she smiles so beautifully it takes my breath away. Is this love, it certainly feels like that because I am not fucking Ella Quinn, I am on a journey of the soul.

I gently rock inside her as we stare into each other's eyes. Neither of us in any hurry to break this spell even for a minute. It feels so right, as if she was made for me and now I know what I've been missing all my life – her. I felt it as soon as she first answered me back and loved the storm in her eyes when she looked at me with contempt. I love every delicious part of Ella Quinn and now she's under me and inside me, I doubt I'll ever be the same again. But how? How can I let her into my world? Would I ever be that selfish? I wasn't kidding when I said I'd ruin Ella Quinn. What I didn't know was the one who would be ruined the most was me.

CHAPTER 20

ELLA

I think I'm in Heaven. I never knew sex could be so good. It's as if it's a drug. Lucas has corrupted me for anyone else—ever. It's not this place, this magical place that could be in the Twilight Zone, it's so far removed from reality I almost expected to see a unicorn strolling majestically down the path with a fairy on its back. Instead, I found Utopia when Lucas invaded my body. My feelings are intense, I never knew I was capable of feeling so hard, but I do. Just being skin on skin with him, closer than I've ever been to a man before, emotionally rather than physically, makes things different.

I've had sex before, but nothing like this. This is something else, and even when he pulls out, I'm hungry for more.

Lucas pulls me into the lake and we start all over again. We make love inside the lake and on its side. He tastes and samples every inch of me, and I have never orgasmed as hard as I do with him. I've lost count of the condoms that lie discarded on the side and time has no meaning as we do everything we shouldn't in a place that nobody knows exists.

It's as if actions have no consequences here. Nothing

matters but the sins of the flesh and the joining of bodies. It's a strangely liberating experience as we frolic in the secret garden like Adam and Eve, devouring each other like wild animals. But I know this is temporary, and I'm under no illusion this is just a distraction to him, a way to pass an afternoon because I see it in his eyes. There's regret in those eyes, something that's bothering him, and yet I push the doubts away.

I know this is temporary, a moment in time, and I'm fine with that. For now, anyway, because even if it means we never meet again after today, I wouldn't have missed this experience for the world. Money can't buy this particular drug and I'm getting the most I can while it's on offer and at the end of it we will go our separate ways because that is what life has in store for us. I'm not stupid, I'm practical and I know our worlds don't mix, so I do everything I can to enjoy the moment and wait for fate to deliver the low blow she usually throws my way.

We lie on the edge of the lake, gazing into each other's eyes, and Lucas looks the most content since I met him. He keeps on staring at me which could be quite awkward, but I love it. He makes me feel like a queen and I am reluctant to leave this magical place, so when he groans and runs his thumb along my lips, I know I'm not going to like his next sentence just from the look in his eyes.

"We must leave, I have missed at least two meetings and I'm guessing Dixie is mighty pissed right now."

"I'm sorry, Lucas, I've kept you from your work."

He laughs and I love hearing it.

"No, darlin', *I've* kept me from my work because for once I'm doing something for me. Not the business, not anyone else, just for me, and if that gets me in trouble, then I'm fine with it."

I giggle and he grins. "What's so funny?"

"You are. I can't imagine you in trouble with anyone. I'm guessing you play by your own rules and to hell with what people think. You know, you're lucky to have that luxury."

"It's not luck, it's destiny."

He sits up and stares across the lake and looks so sad I wonder about his life. How does someone so young reach this level of power?

Sitting up, I drape my arm around his shoulders and for a moment we sit looking across the lake in silence. After a while, I say tentatively, "Tell me about yourself, do you have any family, do they live here?"

He seems sad as he stares into the distance. "No, I have no family, just Tom and Dixie, Adam too."

My heart physically aches as I whisper, "That's sad. What happened to them?"

For a moment, I think he's going to change the subject. I can tell it's a sore one as he sighs. "They died, it's not a happy tale."

Stroking his neck lightly, I wonder whether to push it, and then he sighs heavily, "We should go."

He stands and pulls me up to face him and then, to my surprise, smiles and the look on his face makes me hitch my breath. It's as if all the worry falls away and he looks so beautiful it mesmerises me.

"Thank you, my little flower, you have made me look differently at things."

"Me?"

I am genuinely confused, and he nods. "I may have everything money can buy, but I don't have anything near as valuable as you. Perhaps you should stay."

His words cause something surprising to flare up inside me, and it shocks me more than what he just said. I want to stay, more than anything I want to be with him, never leave and not because of what he owns but because of how he makes me feel.

Then he says sadly, "I wish I could keep you, but it wouldn't be fair."

"On who?"

I am genuinely confused, and he looks so defeated I wonder what happened in his life to make him so wrapped in shadows.

"You Ella, this life, it's dark, intense and destructive. If I dragged you into my world, it would only be a matter of time before you were ruined. It's why I prefer to live alone. To close the world out as much as possible, because why would I want to inflict this prison on anyone else? Especially not someone like you. Maybe it's best if we end this now. Carry on as we were before either of us gets hurt."

"Are you kidding me?"

I feel so hurt by his words and turn away and hate the fact he doesn't try to stop me. The tears blind my eyes as I reach for my clothes and where I was so deliriously happy one minute, I am broken the next.

I try desperately hard not to cry because he has gone from making me feel like the most desirable woman in the world to the cheapest.

To make matters worse, he doesn't appear to care as he dresses quickly and snaps, "Come, we should go."

He is retreating into his hard shell and keeping me out, and I wonder what made him change in the blink of an eye. Was this just about sex, did he use me back there because it certainly feels that way? As I struggle to keep up with him, I feel so betrayed. How could he ruin our perfect moment by making me feel so disposable? I don't think I can ever forgive him for that.

CHAPTER 21

LUCAS

*M*y world is closing in on me and I'm struggling to breathe. Just for a moment back there, I let my guard down and Ella stepped inside. As soon as I saw her looking so innocent, so trusting and so beautiful, it broke me. I can't do this; it's why I fuck whores because I can't open my heart. I will never allow myself to feel again because I just can't deal with the pain that comes with it. I am such a fucking bastard for a reason and I need to protect Ella from that, so I do what's necessary and make her hate me. It's easier this way.

We make it back into the resort and I know she is struggling to understand my change of mood. She's hurt, disappointed and I'm sorry about that but what she doesn't realize is that I'm saving her, setting her free and guaranteeing her safety because if she stayed by my side, she would end up dead. It's a fact that I've had to live with, but I'll be damned if I drag her down with me.

We make our way to my office and Dixie meets us, looking worried.

"Sir, you have three meetings waiting. I've tried to stall

them, but Emmerson Parker is getting antsy and threatening to leave.

Sighing, I say irritably, "Where is he?"

"In the boardroom, sir."

"Fine, I'll head there and keep it short, tell the others I won't be long. Hopefully, I should be able to wrap this up quickly."

She nods and turns away and Ella makes to follow her and I snap irritably, "Where do you think you're going?"

She looks surprised and I say shortly, "Follow me and sit in the corner. I'm not letting you out of my sight."

I turn my back on her and hate myself more than she must right now because I am tearing down something so special that meant way more to me than I'm letting on and I fucking hate every minute of it.

I don't even look at her because I'm guessing I won't like what I'll see, so I head to the boardroom and sweep inside, my hand outstretched. "Emmerson, please forgive me, something came up."

I resist the urge to laugh at the irony as he says angrily, "You're just lucky I'm still here. I've waited for 90 minutes already and that's 89 more than you deserve."

For all his anger, we both know he would wait 24 hours if he had to. It's a known fact that any meeting with me is a triumph. A way to make more money and a way to be accepted in the circles most would kill to be a member of. I could have shifted this meeting onto Adam, but we both know that wouldn't go down well. I am the prize, the golden goose, and I feel a little uncomfortable when I recall the slightly bitter look in Adam's eye when he mentioned that only today.

As I settle down to business, I'm conscious of Ella sitting quietly in the corner. She is writing furiously into her notebook, and I doubt I'd like the words on the page. I almost can't concentrate because there is so much I want to say to her but can't. She must hate me; it's best that way, but I can't deal with the feelings I have toward her and there's nothing I can do about it. She's here for as long as Ryder says she is and I'm stuck with facing my biggest mistake until he says different.

True to my word, I wrap up the meeting inside of twenty minutes and Emmerson leaves looking happy. So he should, because he has just secured a deal for millions of dollars when I agreed to authorize his license for a casino he's building in Atlantic City. As casino's go, it's on the smaller side, but we all need to start somewhere and it's important to allow new growth. Everything changes so quickly these days and becomes more innovative, more luxurious and even more profitable as time goes by and it's necessary to be ahead of the game.

I buzz Dixie and ask her to show the next victim in, and this time it will be a very different conversation.

Damian Reed enterprises is a business I hate doing business with. Outwardly respectable, but behind the façade is a den of iniquity. Drugs, prostitution and illegal gambling. He is here because he wants a legitimate front for his growing empire and thinks I'm going to give it to him—he's wrong. I'm almost tempted to send Ella away from this one because she won't like what she sees, but then again, she *needs* to see this. The ugly side of business that I deal with on a daily basis.

Dixie knows what's coming more than anyone, and she sends in my security team to sit in the far corner of the room. Charlie and Eddie are two of my more trusted guards and they blend into the business as if they're executives, but they hide a deadly skill that many get to witness first hand.

Ella looks up in surprise as they take up their positions

before Dixie shows a beaming Damian Reed into the room, closely flanked by two of his team.

It's obvious one of them is his bodyguard, just by the look of him and the way he checks out my own with a professional detachment. It's like a pissing contest in here already as the atmosphere changes and even Ella sits straighter and looks a little nervous. My heart is screaming at me right now to make her safe. Send her to Dixie and remove her from a potentially toxic situation, but I need her to see this, hell, I need her scared shitless for this to work. To drive her out and make her regret the day she ever met me.

Damien holds out his hand but I ignore it, a move that has him arrowing his eyes and I motion him to sit.

"I'm sorry to keep you waiting, Damien, but business sometimes has its own agenda."

"Then let's cut straight to the chase, Mr. Emiliano, do we have our license?"

"No."

I lean back and the tension in the air closes in on us as his eyes flash angrily. "May I ask why? I have followed the rules to the letter. On what grounds are you refusing me?"

"Damien, let me spell it out for you." I lean forward. "We both know there is nothing wrong with your application on paper. It ticks all the boxes and some more besides. Outwardly it's a good proposition, hell you even threw in a charity foundation for homeless addicts. The governor of our state is on board and you have the backing of several well-appointed businesses. So, I congratulate you on that, but my reach is wide, and it's the business behind it that has sealed your fate."

"What business?" He is actually going to do this—play me for a fool and I snarl, "The prostitution, the illegal gambling, and the drugs. Not to mention the human trafficking that makes me sick to my stomach. How long before that business drags down your respectable one? How can I condone such an operation, I can't?"

"What are you talking about, you know nothing, and if you are calling me out on it, then where's your proof?"

He is so confident I have nothing on him, no tangible evidence linking him to the business behind closed doors. He has always covered his tracks so carefully it's just a shame I have such good friends behind me who can sniff out shit in a nanosecond. Without saying a word, I open the file on the desk that Dixie has prepared and remove several photographs that show him in a very awkward light. There are stills of him indulging in his dubious pursuits, statements from women who have been rescued from his operation. A whole fucking book of depravity that has been researched by the very best and his name is the one on every fucking page.

As he starts reading, I see the penny drop and the bitterness grow in his eyes as he realizes I have so much heat on him, I'm surprised he's not dust already and I wonder how he'll play this. To his credit, he maintains his cool and pushes the papers back to me and snarls, "You've been busy. If I wasn't so angry, I'd be impressed."

I say nothing and as he leans back, he pointedly looks across at Ella and then back at me and I struggle to maintain my cool. He can't see what she means to me, and I only hope he thinks she's just another faceless assistant. He will be keeping his words guarded because he won't want another witness to his failure, and yet I don't miss the meaning in his eyes. I'm used to that. Many people threaten me; think they have an idea how to break me. Blackmail me, bring me down, manipulate me. It's why I live like I do. They have shit on me and one sign of weakness, one hint there is something that could cause my empire to crash and burn they hunt for it like the desperate men they are.

Ella, to her credit, looks bored shitless and won't even

look at me and for the first time I am glad about that and as if testing the water, Damien addresses his next sentence to her.

"Honey, run and fetch me a coffee, be a good girl."

I feel my anger brewing as he speaks to her like a slave and she nods. "Anyone else?"

She looks at everyone but me and totally disregards the tense atmosphere in the room.

As she jumps up, she has to pass him and the bastard leans back and slaps her ass as she passes and I swear time stands still as I feel a blaze of fury burn me up inside. I think Ella is lost for words as she turns and stares at him, and I can feel her anger from across the room. "Did you just really do that?"

Her voice is tightly controlled fury and Damien ignores her and watches me closely for my reaction. I lean back and smirk as if I couldn't give a fuck and say evenly, "Miss. Quinn, you may get the coffee and you have my full permission to drown him in it. Make sure it's hot, it will make him squeal louder."

His eyes narrow as I make him look an idiot and Ella hisses, "Asshole."

I'm not sure if she's talking about him, or me as she storms from the room and Damien smirks. "I love a wild one. You're a lucky man."

I shrug, "Tell that to her boyfriend."

I point to Charlie, who doesn't even blink as he fixes Damien with a thunderous look and makes to stand.

"Show Damien and his group out please, Charlie, our business is concluded."

Damien looks at me angrily, "I haven't finished."

"Yes, you have, request denied, good day."

Charlie and Eddie stand, and Damien looks at his own guard angrily. Obviously, he knows better than his boss and shakes his head slightly. I can feel Damien's frustration as he scrapes back his chair and leans across the table making for the file and I say darkly, "I wouldn't do that if I were you, just leave, we're done."

I almost think he's going to pull his gun on me as his hand twitches and moves to his jacket but a soft click in the corner of the room tells us both my guards have him covered and he shouts, "Fine, I'll go but this isn't over, I'll…"

I snarl, "You'll do nothing. You'll crawl back under your rock and carry on as you were, and you're just lucky I don't turn this file over to the authorities. If I hear your name, or see your face near any of my organizations in the future, then this file drops into the lap of the biggest bastard out there. So, fuck off Damien, request denied and don't make me regret not turning you in today."

We both know I've won; I always do, and as he storms from the room, I breathe a sigh of relief. Another unsatisfied customer to add to the pile of people with a vendetta against me. Life sucks being me, which is why Ella needs to be sent home as a matter of priority.

CHAPTER 22

ELLA

I am so angry. That man was a pig and Lucas just sat there unconcerned and unemotional. Those men are pigs and the whole world's a pig, and if I've learned anything today, it's that I hate them all.

I grit my teeth as the kettle boils and briefly consider taking the elevator and heading home. I'm pretty certain no one would stop me, but there is something keeping me here. It's him - Lucas, the man who has ruined me and carried on with his day and I hate myself for my weakness because I'm not strong enough to do something I must. Leave.

Dixie finds me pacing the small kitchen and the sympathy in her eyes causes the tears to enter mine and to my surprise she steps forward and pulls me in for a hug.

"It's ok, honey, let it all out."

For a moment I'm tempted because this small act of kindness is going a long way right now but I just take some long, deep breaths and say sadly, "How do you deal with this? Those men, Lucas, the power play and dirty talking?"

"And there I was thinking this was quite an easy day."

She laughs softly and I shake my head. "These men are, well, disgusting. Do you know what that…"

"Which one?"

She rolls her eyes and I sigh. "That Damien guy is seriously vile. Do I really have to go back in there?"

"Probably, but I'm guessing he's left already. Lucas will have dispatched him quickly enough. He's on a deadline, after all."

At the mention of Lucas, my face must fall and Dixie sighs. "Don't think badly of him, honey, he's actually one of the good guys, he just forgets that sometimes."

"I can't work him out, Dixie. One minute he's fun to be around, kind, good company and a man that interests me, the next he's cold, rude and a bastard really."

Dixie nods. "He has to be. Listen, I've worked with him long enough to know most of it's a front. It's what makes him so successful. He needs to be cold, a bastard, and it kind of goes with the job. Give him time because I'm guessing he's in new territory right now and is probably struggling to deal with that."

"In what way?"

"You. He's never spent longer than two hours with any woman to my knowledge in the past. If he uses them to escort him to functions, he does everything he can not to have an actual conversation with them. If he uses them for sex, they spend time in his bed and are then sent on their way. He has never taken a woman to his apartment before, let alone had them to stay. He's in a different place with you and we had hoped…"

"What?"

"That you would be the one he needs; to be the person we are rooting for, the woman who will crack the shell he lives behind because Lucas is drowning in the past and there is nobody around to save him."

"What do you mean?"

Dixie looks sad. "It's not for me to say. Lucas is the second most important man in my life and I will never speak out of turn. I love that man like a brother which is a strange thing to say when he's such a bastard most of the time, but when you crack him, he's fiercely loyal and the kindest person I have ever known. It's why we protect him and why we let him control our lives."

"You and Tom."

She nods. "We love him like family and we're all he has. We were both kind of hoping you would join us, so word of advice, whatever he says or does, read between the lines. He will push you away, but only if you let him. I'm not saying it will be easy because you probably want to kill him right now but please, try at least, don't let him push you away, he needs you."

"How do you know; he has made it obvious he's bored already?"

"If he was bored, you wouldn't be here now. I know you're here for your own protection, he told us that at least, but Lucas has an empire and it would be easy for him to protect you without having to live with you. Ask yourself why he insists on watching you every hour of the day, ask yourself why he can't bear to let you out of his sight? It's because he wants you by his side, which tells me everything I need to know. He's struggling and him pushing you away is a reaction to that. Be strong, Ella, and if you want him, fight for him because if you manage it, he will be the best thing to ever happen to you."

She smiles and says kindly, "We should get back. He has one more meeting and then I'm guessing you need to eat. Chalk this one up as a bad day at the office. Take some time to get your head straight, sleep on it, and start a new day clear of the past. If you ever need to talk, both Tom and I know more than most how frustrating he can be. Trust us and trust no one. It will get you through."

She heads off with a wry smile and I think on our conversation. Now I've cooled down a little, I can see her words make perfect sense. Yes, Lucas is struggling, I kind of guessed that, but can I put myself through this mind fuck? I already know the answer, so I sigh and grab the coffee and just wonder if I will end up dousing our disgusting guest in it. Then again, I may be tempted to direct it on Lucas instead after the way he made me feel.

Sighing heavily, I head back into the room.

CHAPTER 23

LUCAS

I am wrapping up my third meeting when Ella heads back into the room. My heart actually sighs with relief when I see her because I wouldn't be surprised if she never came back.

Todd Hardy, the guy from the Vegas Herald is spouting some bullshit about an in-depth interview and I can't get rid of him quickly enough. The fact Dixie arranged this at all has me incensed. I have a PR department for Christ's sake, the last thing I need is a journalist watching my every move, ready to manufacture random crap about my life and everyone in it.

Feeling irritable, I notice Ella clutching the coffee and smile to myself. She is keeping up the pretense even now, and I have to admire her for that. I fix Todd with an impatient look and growl, "I'm sorry Todd, we will need to reschedule. See Dixie on your way out and ask to book a meeting with Heather Daniels, my PR consultant. She will provide you with everything you need."

"But…"

"Good day, Todd."

I stand and he has no choice but to do the same, but I can tell he's pissed. He's probably been bragging to anyone who will listen about his scoop as they call it, and yet I couldn't give a shit. I just need to be with Ella, to make her understand, to protect her and make her safe—from me.

Todd leaves with a fucked off attitude and as the door slams behind him, I turn to Ella.

"Can I expect to be wearing that coffee?"

She looks thoughtful. "You deserve it."

"I know."

For a moment she hesitates, probably planning her words carefully, and then she shakes her head and the hurt expression in her eyes kills my soul.

"Why, Lucas?"

I say nothing and just turn to the window and look out over Vegas. It's a view I've seen a million times and even to me it will never get old. I love it here. I thrive on living here, and yet it's also my own personal hell.

"Ella, you think my life is easy, that I have freedom—I don't."

She perches on the edge of the table and looks at me with interest. "Go on."

I look into her beautiful eyes and see something in them that settles my soul. It's a feeling of contentment, of familiarity that I haven't felt for some time. It's more than sex with Ella, it's her spirit that captivates me and something deep inside me that tells me to hang on tight and never let go. But how can I, how can I put her in danger just to satisfy my own selfish needs?

"You may think I have it all, maybe I did once, but that changed in the most violent of ways."

I'm still in two minds whether to tell her at all, but now I've started, I feel a strange desire to talk about something only Adam has heard before.

"My parents weren't my biological ones. I won't go into the reason I ended up with them, it's something I still can't deal with even after all this time."

My chest heaves because the one nightmare that still haunts me is something I choose not to think about. If I did, I'm not sure I would survive past the day. Some memories are so painful, so bitter, they cut you on every shard that escapes from the impenetrable box you lock them in. Their very existence is like a poison that seeps into your sub conscious and molds your soul. My own personal hell is kept well hidden in a box I am tempted never to open and revisit the time when life changed for me forever.

Some memories are easier to deal with and so I take a deep breath and say sadly, "My father was the Casino King, my mother his queen. They ruled Vegas, and everything I have inherited was their vision. When they adopted me, they gave me everything. Maybe it's because they couldn't have children of their own, but I was loved and adored and molded into their idea of the perfect son."

I smile because I have genuine love for my parents that has never dimmed and Ella's expression is hopeful and her eyes filled with compassion because she knows I'm about to destroy this perfect image with my next sentences.

"I was sent away to the best schools, and I had everything, love, money and a life many can only dream about. When I graduated, I was brought into the company and started on the bottom rung of the ladder to earn my position as the rightful prince to rule by my father's side. It was an exciting time, and I loved it. The power, the responsibility, the fact I was trusted and my opinion mattered. I loved working with my father and never thought it would be any different."

Ella must see the pain enter my eyes and she shifts and heads around the table and to my surprise, sits on my lap and wraps her arm around my shoulders, leaning her head on it and whispering, "It's ok, Lucas, you don't have to open an old wound if it causes too much pain. I understand things haven't been easy for you, you owe me nothing."

My heart almost bursts at this sudden show of kindness. Familiarity that only comes between two people who were made to be together. It's as if Ella is an extension of me—the better part of me and my hand tightens around her waist and I know I need to make her understand.

"We were happy and I have no reason to doubt that, even now. My father was a good man, ruthless but fair and well respected by just about everyone. Then it all changed one weekend."

My heart thumps as that day comes back to haunt me, and I feel a sharp pain where any feeling used to live inside me.

"I was working late and had a visit. The cops came and were escorted in by security. As soon as I saw their faces, I knew it was bad, and they quickly told me my parents had been involved in an accident and it wasn't good. Mom was in theater. She had lost both her legs in the accident and they were battling to save her life. Dad was awake but suffered internal injuries that were life threatening."

"I'm so sorry, Lucas." Ella presses her lips to my neck and tightens her hold and it gives me strength to finish the story.

"I went to the hospital, and it was chaos. There had been a multi-vehicle pileup, and they were caught in it. A tanker had crashed on the interstate and twenty other vehicles were affected. I was helpless, there was nothing I could do, and I had to wait with the rest of them who were as anxious as I was. It felt like days before the doctor came to find me. As soon as he directed me to a private room, something told me it wasn't looking good. It wasn't. Mom hadn't made it. Her injuries were too severe, and strangely my first thought was that she would have wanted it that way. Mom was a fighter, but she wouldn't have coped well living in a wheelchair. She was larger than life and would have hated to be a burden to anyone and not in control of her own life. It hit me hard, and the shock got me through the next 24 hours. Dad was conscious, and the doctor told me I could see him. They hadn't told him about mom and asked if I wanted to be the one to break the news."

Reaching out, I grab the coffee that Ella made and take a long gulp of it. The caffeine helps steady my beating heart as a toxic memory burns inside as if fanned by fate.

"It was hard seeing my powerful father looking so vulnerable. He was broken in spirit and in body and I think somehow he sensed mom was gone because his first words to me were to that effect. 'She's gone.' I just nodded and the tears that were contained by shock found their way to freedom and for the next hour we held hands and cried together for the woman we loved more than life itself."

Ella is crying, I can feel her tears wet against my neck and I lean down and kiss the top of her head. She feels so good in my arms, so familiar, and our connection is strong. I have always known it was because something shifted inside me when she walked into the room, and I wonder if somehow fate delivered her to me for a reason.

"The nurse came in and told me I should leave my father to rest, he still wasn't safe and yet as I stood to leave, he grabbed my hand and whispered, 'I need to tell you something.' The nurse gave us five minutes and left and he asked me to find his wallet. There was something he had to give me. His fingers shook as he brought out the gold coin. The one you copied so exactly."

She stiffens and I can tell she's surprised, but she has to know the implications of why she's here.

"He gave me the coin and told me it was up to me now. He didn't think he'd survive, and just in case, I needed to know. I was to take his place as one of the five kings. An organization that I can never tell you the details of but know that I am one of five members who hold this coin. My father was one, and membership was bestowed rather than applied for. I was to take his place and after his death I would be contacted and all would be explained. It came soon enough. He never survived the night."

"I'm so sorry, Lucas."

Ella's voice is filled with emotion and yet I keep mine locked away. There is no place for it here, so I say in a hard voice. "Both my parents died hours apart, and I was crowned the Casino King by default. Everything I have is down to them and everything I do is because of them. I want to make them proud, make them never doubt their decision to take me in, and so, I need to stay focused. To live in a gilded cage to protect their biggest secret. My life isn't my own, and I am part of a machine that you can only quit in death. That's why you must walk away, Ella, because I don't want this for you. The security, the enemies and the pain. The fact everyone wants a piece of you and any decisions you make have consequences attached. Take Damian Reed as an example. He will think of every way possible to get back at me. Hurt those closest to me, stage an accident, remove me from life and everyone associated with me. I don't have a life, Ella, I have a duty and I don't want that for you. It's why I fuck faceless whores and work every hour I can. It's why I lock myself away with only two people allowed to step inside my world. I trust them, but I don't love them. I treat them well and I treat them just as bad. I don't want that for you, you deserve more than that, so please understand why as soon as Ryder gives us the all clear, I'm setting you free."

CHAPTER 24

ELLA

*L*ucas has devastated me. Just the fact he's opened up and told me something so overwhelming from his past makes me feel trusted, special even, and yet I still don't understand. Why would he turn his back on happiness when his own parents made it through—together? Their accident was just that, an accident. They had a life—a good one.

I turn to face him and to his surprise, kiss him lightly on the lips. Then I pull away and say softly, "They would want you to be happy."

"I know."

He looks resigned to the situation and there's a sadness in his eyes that will probably haunt me forever as he shrugs, "It has to be this way."

I'm not sure I agree with him, but I know whatever I say won't change his mind, so I smile sadly. "Then we had better make the most of the time we do have."

He looks surprised and I smile. "Thank you for telling me, Lucas, but it changes nothing, on my part, anyway. I'm willing to give this—us a chance, but it needs you to want the same. If your decision is to walk away, I'm not going to beg but just know I think we have something worth trying for. It's not the money or the empire that surrounds you, it's you, Lucas. The man who infuriates me and makes me want to smash something—preferably over his head. The man who challenges me and makes me question my own sanity most of the time, but the man I am falling for so hard, the impact will probably break me. I am not in control of my mind right now and in no position to make any decisions. I'm just riding the wave and not keen to go under just yet. So, what do you say, shall we have some fun and make some memories to replace the sad ones we live with because I'm up for that—are you?"

He looks surprised, and yet there's relief in his eyes that warms my heart. I've made him relax; I can see that immediately.

He nods and I see a little of his cockiness return. "Are you sure you can cope with me?"

"Not really, but I'm kind of willing to give it a try. I may have to push back a little though, I do have self-preservation issues I'm trying to develop where it concerns you."

He laughs against my lips and then he kisses me so hard, it sends a message straight to the whore in me and as he pushes my top from my shoulders, I squirm with desire on his lap, feeling his rock-hard cock pressing against my pussy through the fabric of our clothes. I help him off with his own shirt and then with a low growl, he pushes me back on the table and removes my skirt. He kisses my body reaching my thighs and eases my legs apart, exposing me to him in the most depraved of ways. He licks a trail from back to front and then his tongue dips inside as he sucks my clit, causing me to cry out. Laughing, he pulls back and replaces his tongue with his fingers and moves up to kiss my lips so I taste my own arousal on his tongue.

"Do you want me inside you, Ella?"

"Hell, yeah." I laugh softly and he grins wickedly and grabs a condom from his pocket and makes short work of sheathing his cock. Then he plunges in hard and my back scrapes against the polished wood. As I lie with my back on the table, I gaze up at an image of perfection as he pounds inside me, hard and unrelenting.

He stares at me the whole time like a warrior, a conqueror, an alpha male, and as I feel him hard and unforgiving inside me, I feel the pressure build as my body screams its acceptance of being dominated by him. He is hard, relentless and as if he's a caveman claiming his mate and I love every minute of it. I cry out, not even caring if the whole resort can hear us. I'm like a wild animal myself as I bite my lip and groan with desire.

One last thrust has me falling, wildly, deeply and as if I'm about to hit the ground and never be the same again. I will be broken and saved in the same soul shattering fall and whatever happens next is worth this moment. It will always be worth this moment because even if we never do this again, it will be worth every delicious second of it. How can I regret feeling something so amazing, it's doubtful I ever will again? This is the reason I was born—he is the reason I was born, and if we never see each other again, my life is complete.

THE WALK of shame is an interesting one as we leave the boardroom and head to the elevator. Maybe it's my imagination, or my guilty conscience, but it feels as if everyone knows what just went on in there. I wish I could hide my face away from the smirks on the faces of the people who work busily away in their cubicles, and I hate the fact that Lucas obviously thinks nothing of it as he strides ahead.

Then again, I get an uncomfortable feeling when I realize that probably wasn't the first time he did that, and it makes me feel worthless, as if I'm just another one of those 'faceless whores' he fucks and carries on with his day.

I know I'm being irrational; he has never given me cause to think that, but part of me feels it because he isn't promising me a happily ever after, just the door when Ryder King opens it.

We head to his private elevator and as soon as we're inside, he takes my hand and squeezes it. "Stop thinking."

"You can't tell me what to do with my own thoughts now."

He laughs and rolls his eyes. "I know what you're thinking and you're wrong. You mean something to me, Ella, and I'm guessing I mean a lot to you too."

"You're a bit presumptuous, what if I'm just using you for sex?"

He laughs and presses my hand to his already rigid cock. "Then color me happy, darlin' because I kind of love the idea of being a fuck toy, play with me as much as you wish."

I can't help but grin like the village idiot and as the elevator stops, I note with surprise we're back in his apartment and not his office.

"Dinner time." He winks and I realize that food was furthest from my mind and now my stomach growls in approval of this latest turn of events.

We head inside his luxurious penthouse and are greeted by Tom who nods to Lucas and when he's not looking, winks at me.

"Dinner is served, sir."

Lucas nods. "Thanks, Tom, no need to hang around, I'll call you when we're done."

Tom nods respectfully, and I don't miss the slight smile on his face. After Dixie's words earlier it feels good knowing they are rooting for me and I smile, but there's sadness behind it when I realize this is just temporary. Lucas looked so determined about that, and it would take a miracle for him to change his mind.

Pushing away the thought of what that will mean for me, I follow him to the dining room and love the fact Tom has opened the bi-fold doors onto the terrace for us to watch the sun setting in Vegas against a backdrop of candles that burn on every surface. Lucas laughs softly. "Tom is a hopeless romantic, no prizes for guessing what's on his mind."

"I think your staff want you to be happy, even if you don't."

A hint of bitterness creeps into my tone, and I'm angry with myself about that as he stills and shakes his head. "It has to be this way, I told you my reasons."

Ignoring him, I head over to the table that Tom has laden with food and lift off one of the silver domes. "This looks good enough to eat."

Lucas laughs softly, "It had better be, I pay my chef too much to feed me well."

As I help myself, it strikes me how privileged Lucas is. Just imagining my usual ready meal that I flip into the microwave when I return from work, makes me a little envious of his lifestyle. How lovely to have gourmet food on tap when you return weary from work. As I take my seat and feel the cool breeze of a Vegas evening wrap itself around my senses, I sigh. "I wish your chef lived with me; my diet is sorely lacking any nutritional value these days."

Lucas joins me and looks interested. "Tell me about your day."

"Well, I live in an apartment in the university district. It's a rental that stretches me a little, but it's worth it for the security it provides. I work in Copycat most of the day and when I return, I manage a microwave meal for one and then watch Netflix and surf the internet."

"Sounds like luxury living to me."

Lucas smiles, and I know he probably means that. "It must be nice to only have yourself to worry about."

He sounds a little pensive and I nod. "It's fine most of time. I have some friends I call on if I fancy a night out."

"What does that involve?"

I can tell he is hanging onto every word I speak, and I grin. "It usually starts in a bar, ends in a club, and then an argument over whether to continue the evening in a casino. Normally that's when I bail and grab an Uber and head home."

"You don't gamble then."

"I told you, I can't afford the consequences of that. You see, Lucas, I work hard for my money—really hard. Why would I want to piss it down the drain to make you richer? We both know that's what would happen in the end. No, I'm too savvy for that because I am saving for a little house in a nice town somewhere by the sea. I want the dream and Copycat is going to make that happen."

"It sounds as if you're on the right track, I mean, $200,0000 dollars is a lot of money, easily enough for a down payment on a house."

"I told you, I spent it already."

"On what?"

He seems surprised and I shake my head. "Mom's nursing care is expensive, and I wanted a place as amazing as she is. It doesn't come cheap, and then there were Hannah's medical bills."

"Tell me about her."

Lucas appears hungry for information and as I tell him about my family, my life and every boring detail, he listens as if I am the most interesting person alive.

It's only when I reach the part about them wanting to set me up with one of Evan's friends, that his eyes darken and he seems seriously pissed off.

"What's the matter, Lucas, you've gone quiet on me."

"Have I? I thought listening was a life skill."

"I can think of other more exciting life skills that I kind of think you've mastered."

I try to lighten the atmosphere and he grins, his eyes flashing wickedly.

"Maybe you would like me to teach you some more."

"I thought you'd never ask."

Lucas grins and just like that he's back—the wicked player who was born to corrupt my soul.

As he reaches for my hand, I feel a shiver of desire inside.

Tonight should be interesting.

CHAPTER 25

LUCAS

The next few days are spent indulging my new love of Ella. She appears to accept the situation, and I'm not sure if I'm happy about that. It makes things easier but every time I touch her, kiss her, fuck her and taste her, I am sliding down a rabbit hole that I know leads to a dead end. The only outcome of this will be her leaving me. I am preparing myself for that; she is preparing her for that, and yet we both dread the day it happens.

It's not an option to change things, I know that it's best for her if I cut her free. The selfish part of me wants to keep her by my side and make a future with her, something I never thought I had. But every time that delicious thought rears its head, a thousand faces push it away again. Damian Reed, for one. The way he looked at her told me she wasn't safe. The way anyone would look at her would have me checking over my shoulder with fear every hour of the day because Ella is fast weaving her spell around my heart and having lost so many people I love, I just can't go through that again.

Then there's this life—not just the empire I've built, but

the one only a select few know about. It's ok for Ryder King, he has it all. A loving family, a wife, kids and a set of friends who would die for him. It's the nature of his business to protect them, and I know nothing would ever harm them. Ryder is the one King who has this luxury. The lucky one among us which is possibly why he was targeted when the gold coin was copied. It still confuses me as to who would set him up that way? Surely, it's an uneducated mistake because if Ryder finds out who it was, they have met their maker the moment he reaches them. Someone with a death wish, or a lot to gain by his demise. When he told me of the trap they were lured to, my blood ran cold. Life without Ryder would be impossible for us all, which makes me even more nervous about bringing Ella into this life.

But she's here already, and for some reason I am anxious about letting her leave. She has fallen into this one way or another, but will she ever be completely safe? It's the part of me that is conflicting with my resolve. I need to trust Ryder to get to the bottom of this because until he does, none of us are safe.

$\sim$

THIS MORNING I have a breakfast meeting with Adam, so I leave Ella to sleep off the effects of the night before. I am insatiable where it concerns her, and I'm not sure sleep featured much during the night.

I just can't get enough of her, but every second I'm inside her, I am preparing myself to leave. I know it's temporary, maybe that's what makes it so desirable. Knowing that the one thing I want the most is out of my control, I can't have it because I think too much of her to ruin her life for something I want above anything else.

"Hey, you look a lot better. Having a house guest obviously agrees with you."

Adam grins as I head into the boardroom where Tom has arranged a working breakfast. It's 7am and I feel so good despite the lack of sleep and I'm hungry to get my business wrapped up so I can lose myself inside Ella for the rest of the day.

"She's a diversion, I'll give you that."

Adam grins and I hate the way those words tasted. He can't know how I feel about her, nobody can because that will safeguard her future.

"So, before we get down to business, Penelope told me to ask you to brunch on Sunday."

I raise my eyes and he shakes his head and sighs. "Just so you know, she's invited half the socialites of Vegas. The fact you're on the guest list will make it the hottest ticket in town and she's counting on me securing her position as head bitch. So, do me a favor and spare us an hour at least."

I stare at him in surprise because this isn't like Adam. He's not the kind of guy to care what his wife wants, especially when it concerns me.

He squirms a little and sighs. "Listen, you know I hate to ask, it's just that my life would be much easier if Penelope's happy. She's on edge these days and I'm not sure what's going on."

"Have you asked her?" I don't usually do marriage guidance, but something is affecting my right-hand man and that concerns me. He's unhappy. A fool could see that and I'm pretty sure newlyweds aren't meant to look so jaded after only six months of wedded bliss.

"Of course, but she tells me she's trying to forge a position for us in this town as a couple. She has reminded me it's hard on her having left Boston to come here and start again.

She had a promising career there and now she's just somebody's wife and she's struggling."

"Then give her a child; that will keep her busy."

Adam laughs. "You don't know, Penelope. If she wants a child, it will be planned for accordingly. Nothing will be left to chance, and I'm not sure I'm ready for that nightmare just yet. All I want is to enjoy fucking her senseless when I return home at night and having someone who listens to my endless whining about what a bastard my boss is."

He laughs as I raise my eyes. "Sounds like you need a whore more than a wife. Not exactly my idea of a happy marriage."

"Says you, the self-styled bachelor who won't even date, let alone marry. Maybe you should try it and then you'll understand where I'm coming from."

He turns his attention to the food and I think on his words. Would I do anything for Ella if she asked, even if it set my teeth on edge? Would I go against what I want just to make her happy? I already know the answer to that, and so I feel a flash of sympathy for Adam and groan.

"I'll be there. What time?"

"Thanks, Lucas." His voice is rough around the edges and woven with relief, and I can tell this was the most important deal on his agenda today.

Thinking back to the weary eyes, the beaten aura and the bitterness in his eyes, I wonder when he changed. I can only think it happened a few months after his wedding. Adam is struggling, it's obvious, and his wife is the reason.

"I'm bringing Ella, though." I throw it out there and he laughs. "I thought you might."

"Why?"

"Because you've changed since she came here. I never really bought your story about her as your assistant. What's the real story?"

145

I carefully consider my words because Adam's no fool and I shrug.

"It's true, she is Dixie's replacement. The trouble is, as it's a temporary position, I thought I'd take your advice and relieve some of the tension that's been building. She's an attractive diversion and so yes, I'm fucking my assistant for as long as she stays here. It's convenient and makes the day more interesting, so does that answer your question?"

I hate every word that just came from my mouth because I meant none of them. I feel like a bastard even talking about her this way and as Adam grins and leers, "You have good taste, I may have been interested myself back in the day. God knows I've done the same thing myself on many occasions."

Resisting the urge to blast that smirk off his face with my gun, I say tersely, "Anyway, what was so urgent you called this meeting?"

Suddenly, the mood changes and Adam looks worried, which unnerves me more than I let on.

He pushes his plate away and seems edgy and then lowers his voice to a whisper.

"The project is threatened."

"What, Silver City?"

"Yes."

"But why?" I'm surprised because Silver City is central to my plans going forward. As big as Disneyland, this place is set to be the home of gaming outside of Vegas. Condos, shops, casinos and hotels, all set around a town that will thrive. A mini state in itself, my life's dream, and I plan on making it the most desirable place in the world to visit.

Adam looks worried. "I heard word that the markets edgy. Bill told me word on the street is it's set up to fail. Investors are pulling out as the cancer spreads and there has been a few calls from the bank threatening to pull the plug unless we can turn the bad publicity into good."

"The banks?" I stare at him incredulously because I fucking own those dirty bastards and they wouldn't dare go against me.

Adam sighs. "I'm sorry, Lucas, I thought you should know. Things aren't looking good and the market is jittery. Share prices are tumbling and we're struggling."

"Based on what?" I bring my fist crashing down on the table and Adam jumps. "Based on bad press and poisoned words. You know how this works; a few whispered lies and it costs millions. I thought you had contacts on Wall Street; that you had people on the stock exchange working to your benefit. Maybe you should call in a few favors because your whole empire could be about to crash and burn."

His words fly around me like bullets from a gun. Each one causing multiple wounds in a fractured ego.

As his words find their target, I feel the fury burning inside as the repercussions of our conversation begin their fatal path.

Adam looks concerned as I growl, "This meeting has ended."

"But..."

"Fuck off, Adam, this is in my hands now. Get back to work and do some digging. Find out who is badmouthing us and discover the weak link in our organization. Leave nothing untouched and report back every single fucking conversation you hear. If something or someone is set on bringing me down, they will pay dearly."

Adam looks shit scared as he leaves the room and I'm not surprised. I rarely get angry, but when I do, the gambling world shakes in terror and the fault lines it creates reach far and wide.

As I reach for my cell, there's only one number I need to call and he better have answers for me because if he's not behind it, then we are all fucked.

CHAPTER 26

ELLA

*W*hen I wake, Lucas is gone, and for a moment I feel lost. I'm not sure when I became used to him being around. If he's not beside me, I feel the emptiness and I frown a little. This isn't good. I know the clock is ticking, I'm on borrowed time here. He's made that perfectly clear, but it doesn't mean I have to like it.

Just for a minute, I lie in his silken sheets and stare around the room at more luxury than I ever thought I'd see in my life. The trappings of wealth and having everything in life, except for one thing—true happiness. Lucas may have everything money can buy, but he is poor where it counts. His family died—tragically and I'm not sure if he ever really came to terms with that.

My heart breaks for him because just thinking about how close I came to losing my sister, how I live with the knowledge mom doesn't have long, makes me feel raw pain inside. How will I cope when mom does pass and how long does Hannah really have? We never knew our father, he died when we were small girls. It was a short illness and I suppose we were lucky not to live through that, but I don't think mom ever fully recovered.

Having met Lucas, I kind of know how hard love can hit you. It's why I'm trying my best not to fall too heavy because I'm in no doubt I have fallen—hard and it's the man, not the wealth that interests me the most.

Deciding to grab a shower, I indulge myself in some quiet time while I have it. Most of my time with Lucas appears to consist of him inside me, and I'm not complaining about that. I know he's desperate. To feel while he can. He is an empty shell and won't allow anyone in, I kind of understand why, no matter how I wish things were different.

The shower revives me and I wrap myself in a silken robe and wander through his amazing apartment, taking in every detail and committing it to memory. I never really knew people lived like this. It's like something from a movie, but it's Lucas's life and if I wasn't so sad for him, I'd be impressed.

"Hey, Ella, lovely morning."

I look up and smile as Tom heads into the room, pushing a cart laden with food.

"Morning Tom, you've been busy."

I laugh as he buckles under the weight of the feast he has arranged and he grins.

"I never know what you prefer, so I bring everything."

"Maybe you should let us order and then it wouldn't be so wasteful."

He shrugs. "It's not wasted and most of it is used in some way. Mainly by me when you've finished."

He laughs and I smile. "So, tell me about you, Tom, what's your life like outside the glass bowl?"

I watch as he sets up the table and he shrugs. "I have it good, Ella. Mostly Lucas isn't around and my days are my own to arrange. I love taking care of him and when I'm not, I have friends I catch up with, my own apartment to maintain and family I visit."

"Is your apartment far?"

"On the floor below."

I'm surprised and it must show because he nods. "I have a large apartment and Dixie has another. Charlie and Eddie also have neighboring ones because Lucas likes to keep his staff close. He's a very generous boss when he's not being a bastard to the masses and we have it good compared to most."

"What will Dixie do when she's married?"

"I'm not sure, I don't think any of us have really thought this through. I mean, her 'husband to be' is successful in his own right and won't want to move in here. He has his own house and life and will expect her in it. I think Lucas is dreading the day Dixie leaves because he will have the inconvenience of training somebody else."

"I can see your problem."

Tom shrugs. "There are a few candidates on the horizon, women he has stand in for Dixie when she's on vacation. My preference is Mrs. Evans. She scares the pants off me and Lucas if he'll admit it, and she has no life outside of work to get in the way."

"Who's Mrs. Evans?" I'm quite surprised because she sounds like a school mistress and Tom grins. "She works for Adam because he screwed so many of his assistants, it was becoming obvious one of them would sue one day, so Lucas found Mrs. Evans. Adam was pissed, but the rest of us found it funny. To be honest, she's better than most and certainly gets the job done, which is, after all, what they are paid to do. She also idolizes Lucas for some reason, won't hear a bad word said about him, and keeps Adam firmly in check. I'm guessing she will get the job if Dixie ups and leaves, heading off for her happily ever after."

"And you, Tom, what about you, is there someone special you go home to?"

"I have a guy I see, but it's just casual. Nothing serious, he travels a lot because he's a flight attendant, which suits me just fine. I'm not ready to settle down. Why would I when I'm living the dream?"

He pours me a coffee and I smile my thanks, taking a seat and saying, "Will you join me, it feels odd eating alone?"

"Girl, I'd be honored."

He takes his seat opposite and grabs a coffee for himself and it feels good to have company. It's only now I realize how empty my own life is, and Tom looks concerned.

"You've got a sad look in your eye, Ella, what's the matter, I'm a good listener?"

"Sorry." I shake my head. "I was just thinking about my own life. I live alone you see and most of the time it's just me. I also work alone, so I kind of understand Lucas. It's not what should happen. Humans aren't designed to live alone even though I value my space."

"Don't you have a boyfriend?"

"No, not really. I have dated a few guys that I met either as customers or online, but they never really go anywhere."

"And Lucas?" Tom leans forward looking interested and I blush a little, making him laugh. "It's ok, honey, nobody would blame you for going there. After all, we've all had those fantasies, that man's a god."

We giggle and I say sadly. "We both know my stay here is temporary. Lucas has made that perfectly clear. To be honest, I'm not sure I'm cut out for this life, anyway. I like to work, live with freedom, and not have people shadow my every move. I know they're discreet but those body-guards follow Lucas everywhere, it's a little overwhelming, really."

Tom looks sad. "It has to be that way. When you're at the

top of your game, the numero uno, everyone is out to bring you down."

He leans in and lowers his voice to a whisper. "You know, Lucas will never say, but word on the street is his folk's accident wasn't as it seemed."

"Really."

Tom nods. "Some say it was orchestrated, and they were always the intended victims. This is why Lucas lives in a bullet proof world. He's had a tragic life, and it probably won't get any better. It's why we do everything we can to make him happy because it's painfully obvious he's not—happy that is."

We hear the elevator and Tom stands and winks. "My cue to leave, enjoy your day, Ella, anything you need just holler."

Tom smiles as Lucas heads into the room, and I immediately know his meeting didn't go well by the storm in his eyes and the frown on his face.

Tom also notices and throws me a pitying look as he says pleasantly, "Can I get you anything, sir?"

Lucas looks a little distracted and shakes his head. "No, thank you, Tom, I'll call if I need anything."

As Tom leaves, I look at Lucas with concern as he grabs a coffee absentmindedly and looks deep in thought. Something has definitely happened and from the looks of it—it's not good.

CHAPTER 27

LUCAS

I'm not sure what to think after the conversation I've just had with Hunter. If word on the street is unsettling my project, he assured me it didn't come from him. Now we have a problem that will take some solving and rather than head to my desk as I usually do, I've come to the only person I want to be with in a crisis. Ella.

She looks so gorgeous sitting in her silken robe sipping on a mug of coffee. So perfect, delicate and unspoilt and nothing like the toxic air I breathe every day.

I can tell she's concerned and yet I can't let her in, it's not fair on her or the organization I represent.

Sighing, I set the mug down and kneel before her, wrapping my arms around her waist and pulling her close so I can breathe her scent and chase the shadows away. She runs her fingers through my hair and drops light kisses on the top of my head and whispers, "Do you need to talk?"

There is so much I want to say, so much I want to confide in her but how can I? She's a temporary delight that will soon be gone and I can't allow myself the luxury of opening up to someone who will be gone from my life as quickly as she came.

Instead, I just pull her close and savor the time we do have. I know I should be working through my troubles; I should be calling in favors and getting to the root of the problem but not now. I want something more, so I part her robe and love how sweet she smells. How soft her skin is and how good she feels.

I press gentle kisses on her stomach and move my head lower, tasting her sweet essence that always appears ready to delight my senses. As I flick my tongue inside, she groans and I love how powerful that makes me feel. Parting her thighs, I pleasure her as she throbs against me and opens up like a flower. I'm in no hurry to move this on, just enjoying the taste of innocence, of normality and of perfection.

Pulling her legs wide, I suck on her clit and her gentle moans make the beast inside me roar. I can tell she's close, semi-naked in the chair with her legs wide, being eaten out by a desperate man. What a way to start the day, I could get used to this and as she comes apart around me, I love her small squeals of pleasure and the moans of a woman who has reached a satisfying climax.

By the time she gets her breath, I close the robe and drop a light kiss on her lips before smirking. "Morning gorgeous."

"Same. What's up though, you look, well, terrible actually. What's the matter, weren't your eggs to your liking, or your bacon cold?"

Grabbing the seat opposite, I reach for a pastry. "The food was adequate, the conversation poor."

"Do you want to talk about it?"

"Yes and no."

"Make up your mind." She laughs softly and I smile. "Yes, I want to talk about it and no I can't. It's business that will tie me up for most of the day, if not the week. I'm pissed about that because I want to spend my time with you and yet I know this is out of my hands."

I feel so desperate as my coming days look bleak and she reaches across the table and takes my hand. "It's fine, you do what you must, I should get to work, anyway. I have orders building that I need to get out the door and I've been kidding myself that I have the time to spend indulging in pleasure."

Her words hit me like a sledgehammer. "Work, what do you mean?"

She shakes her head sadly. "Lucas, I have a business. *You* have a business. Respect mine, at least. When this all ends, *we* end and I have to pick up the shattered pieces and glue them back together. I accept how it is, I'm just not sure you realize what it could cost me. I will need my business, so I must tend it, nurture it and allow it to grow because ultimately it's all I have. Let me go back to it, let me have my freedom, and I promise you I will be here when you return."

"No!" My voice is loud, and is driven by the sudden panic in my heart. She can't leave, I won't allow it. For some reason, I feel so desperate and want to hold on tight. She can't walk outside, away from me, it's not happening.

Her eyes burn with unshed tears and I feel like the biggest bastard in the world because I won't keep her, but I can't let her go. I'm being selfish, I know I am, but just thinking of her away from me for two seconds is too painful. I like knowing she's here, waiting for me. At my beck and call, a warm body to cling to in an otherwise cold existence. I need Ella, she's the beat of my heart and the life in my body. She can't leave, I won't have it.

Images of me chaining her to my bed and keeping her there, flash before my eyes as the panic sets in, making me an irrational monster. I'm unreasonable, scared and drowning in unfamiliarity and to my surprise, she pushes back her chair and heads around the table and sits on my lap, wrapping her arms around my neck and pressing her lips lightly to mine. I cling on tight as if I can't let her go and she whispers, "It's ok, Lucas, I understand. I'll be here when you are. I promise to be careful and I *will* come back."

My heart is frantic and I'm losing control. What is happening, this isn't like me, I don't lose control, I don't feel. I can't take it and as she nuzzles my neck, she whispers, "I love you, Lucas."

Four words that suddenly change everything.

With a feral growl, I lift her in my arms and stride from the room. I head inside my bedroom and push her down on the bed and rip that robe from her body as if it's nothing. Then I shrug out of my clothes in record time and without any foreplay, plunge inside her body causing her to cry out.

Just feeling her warm body contracting around my cock sends me delirious. It feels so good, so wrong to be bareback inside her and like a perfect paradise. Her legs wrap around my waist and pull me in deeper. She gasps as I pound inside her relentlessly, desperate to mark her, to claim her, to love her in the only way I know how. I want my stamp all over her, inside and out and I suck on her neck like a fucking vampire as I feel a desperate urge to mark my territory. For someone who likes control I well and truly lose it and as I fuck Ella Quinn into the mattress, I come so hard I roar like the beast I am with no care for the consequences.

CHAPTER 28

ELLA

*H*e's out of control. I should be scared, but how can I be? Lucas Emiliano is a man who feels nothing but feels too much. He can't cope with losing control and is doing the only thing he can. He's a dominant, a man who likes to conquer, manipulate and call the shots. I saw the panic in his eyes when I asked to leave. He doesn't want to keep me, but he can't bear the thought of me walking away. That sparked a tiny flame of hope inside me. We could make this work; I know we can but not on his terms. It has to be on mine, and the only way to save Lucas is to leave him.

The fact he's just fucked me raw excited me way more than it should. He came so hard inside me and I don't give a fuck. It felt good feeling his seed coating me inside. Running down my legs and marking me with his scent. I now own a part of him he has never given another because he is the condom King, I know that at least, but not now, not with me and it's just lucky I'm on birth control because that's a complication I am unwilling to face.

He collapses on top of me and holds on tight, and I feel

his heart beating against mine as he faces the consequences of what just happened. Stroking his back lightly, I kiss his shoulder and he whispers, "I'm sorry, Ella."

"For what?"

"For acting like a fucking caveman."

I giggle and whisper, "I kind of love a caveman."

Pulling back, he smirks into my eyes and I love seeing his wicked look.

He's back.

The scared, lost look has gone and the cocky bastard has returned.

"Sorry about the mess."

He grins as we feel the sticky results of what just happened cementing us together and I shake my head. "I kind of like that too."

His eyes shine as he kisses my lips lightly and then whispers, "About your business."

"What about it?"

My heart beats wildly as I wait for his words and he smiles. "I'm being an asshole. Of course, you need to tend to it. We'll move it here instead."

"No." I stare at him with a hard look and he looks surprised.

"I have a shop. I need people to be able to come in off the street. How will I get customers if they have to wander through layers of security just to make an enquiry? You're not thinking this through."

He looks angry and rolls off me and I say gently, "I'll be fine. Trust me."

"I do, Ella, but unless you've forgotten, you're not safe. This hasn't just ended you know, the threat is still there."

"I'll be fine."

Sighing, he leans on his side and looks me in the eye.

"Compromise. You go back and sort out your shit. Complete any orders you have and make arrangements to deliver. Then close up for as long as this takes and I will make up the revenue lost. If you go, you take security with you. My men will make sure it's safe and watch over you. Non-negotiable, it's that or nothing."

For some reason this feels like a victory and I nod. "We have a deal."

He seems to breathe a little easier and looks as if he's just weathered a storm.

"Good, I'll make the arrangements and have a car available to you. You can work while I work and then you're mine in the evenings."

I smile, but I feel a sadness inside that just won't go away. This may be a temporary fix, but there's still the realization this is a ship that's waiting to sail. All we're doing is postponing the inevitable and yet that suits me because I can't bear the thought of leaving him even for a minute and if this is gradual removing of the sticking plaster, then I'll take it because I'm in no hurry to leave him, anyway.

Two hours later and I'm on my way. It feels strange leaving the casino. Wearing my usual clothes and walking outside into the daylight. Lucas insisted I hand over my keys to his guards, who left almost immediately to check it was safe. Now I am being accompanied by Charlie to work, in a bullet-proof car. It feels so strange, nothing like an ordinary girl like me would ever normally experience, and yet I'll take it if it means I get back to work.

As soon as we pull up outside Copycat, I feel the tears burn. It feels as if I've been away for months, years, even instead of a few weeks. It looks smaller somehow, a little shabby even, and yet it's home and my heart bursts as I regain a little control of my life.

I wait for Charlie to check it's clear and resist the urge to roll my eyes. I know Lucas is being overprotective, and I kind of understand why. How can I judge him when I don't walk in his shoes? It must be hard for him and makes me understand a little of his life and why he is so protective of it.

Luckily, he has a lot to occupy him and could probably do with me being out of his space, anyway. I know he's worried about everything it seems, and a little distance will make things easier—on us both.

As soon as I step inside my shop, my world rights itself. I'm back and it feels so good. Maybe I'm happier because I know I'm heading back to Lucas at the end of the day. It feels good knowing he's there for me, waiting and promising me an evening of more pleasure than a body can surely stand.

Charlie seems like a good guy and he smiles. "It's all clear, Miss. Quinn."

"Please call me Ella." I smile and he relaxes a little.

"Ella."

"So, Charlie, this is going to be a bit boring for you, so why don't I make you a coffee and set up a movie or something on my iPad?"

"No need, Ella, I can make the coffee and I wouldn't dream of any distractions while I do my job."

He winks and I smile to myself. Of course, they are never off duty; I wonder how they cope with the boredom.

I turn my attention to business and groan when I see the orders piling up. The result of taking a few weeks off is coming back to bite me, and as I make my way through the list, I can tell it's going to be a busy afternoon. Really, I should work long into the night to get them done, but I promised Lucas I would be back by 7pm at the latest and it wouldn't be fair on Charlie to keep him hanging around that long.

So, as he takes up residence on the front desk, I head out the back and start doing what I do best. Copying things.

CHAPTER 29

LUCAS

*I*t was the right thing to do. Despite the fact I hated every second arranging Ella's departure from my side, I know she needs to work and so do I. What happened with Adam is still raw. There's a spanner in the works and I need to find out who put it there.

I tried so hard to push Ella from my mind as I worked all morning, sifting through reports, records and articles. I have Dixie and Adam working on finding out information on our backers and trawling through articles online that mention my organizations at all.

The picture building is a concerning one because word on the street is destructive. Hell, I probably wouldn't invest in my own fucking venture if I had half a brain, and I'm not surprised the market is getting cold feet.

I try so hard to blank Ella from my mind but it's impossible, so around lunchtime, I call Tom and instruct him to make up a basket to go and call my car around.

As we pull up outside Ella's business, I look with interest at a rather shabby shop front with an interesting image of a cat looking in a mirror outside.

I wonder about the people who come here. It's a strange business to own and 10/10 for originality. As I grab the wicker basket, I wonder what she'll think of this. To be honest, I'm not sure what I think of this because this is out of character for me. I don't chase women down like a lovesick fool. I fuck them and then they leave. It's always been that way, but there's something about Ella that's special and I kind of like the effect she's having on my life.

Once the coast is clear, Eddie, one of my guards, holds open the door and I head inside.

Charlie looks up from his position at the front desk and nods. "She's out back, Boss."

"Take a break, Charlie, Eddie's got this."

He nods and is probably thanking me right now because he must be bored shitless babysitting because I'm so fucking terrified of anything happening to the woman who has surprised me by showing up in my heart.

I push through the door and see Ella bent over her desk, deep in concentration. She looks up and the surprise on her face makes me laugh as I hold up the basket.

"Lunch."

"Seriously." She shakes her head and I shrug.

"I don't like to eat alone."

"Since when?" Grinning, she sets her pen down and stands and I admire the fact her t-shirt clings to her tits, making me glad I came.

Setting the basket down on the side, I look around with interest.

"So, this is your kingdom."

"Yes, it's not as impressive as yours, but I like it."

Despite the fact it's basic and rather cramped, it looks clean and well-ordered, which tells me a lot about her.

She sits on the corner of the desk and looks at me with interest.

"So, how come you're here? I mean, it's nice and all, but I thought we were keeping a low profile."

"We are."

"Then forgive me for stating the obvious but anyone watching this shop, that's if they are in fact, surely you've just blown your cover by turning up here mob handed, carrying a fucking picnic basket."

She does have a point and I'm impressed.

"True, this may have blown our cover as you say." I laugh softly. "It's why I have operatives stationed at every corner, covering every window in site, and observing from across the street."

She laughs softly. "Is that right?"

Advancing closer, I fix her with a devilish smile. "I needed to check this out for myself. For some reason I couldn't stop thinking of you here, unprotected without me around."

She laughs out loud. "You call this being unprotected. I'm guessing your men have a lot more skill in protection than you do."

"True, but I'm talking here about close protection. None of my men will ever get close enough to you to warrant that title. I mean, if I stand in front of you, they would have to get through me to you, pretty impressive right."

"Maybe, then again, what would that achieve? I mean, surely you are the bigger target, anyway, so their job would be done."

"What a way to go though."

"If you say so." She grins and I dip my head and capture her smile against my lips and she tastes so fucking good. Like the sweetest candy and I'm like a kid who can't get enough as I run my hand around her head and pull her closer, grinding my lips on her in a fevered show of passion. It feels so good to be here with her. Why can't I appear to breathe without her by my side? How has this happened in such a short time, and what the fuck am I going to do about it?

She feels so good, soft and vulnerable as she shivers against me and I'm having a hard time remembering the fact we have close on a dozen operatives outside watching our every move.

Reluctantly, I pull back and nod to the basket.

"So, are you hungry, I brought food?"

"What have you got?"

With a flourish, I open the basket and reveal the wrapped sandwiches, small pots of salad, pasta and dips. Fruits and desserts that make my mouth water and a big bottle of champagne that I proceed to uncork before pouring some into two crystal glasses that are a little over the top but who cares. She deserves the best of everything and I demand it.

We sit on her desk and I look with interest at what she's working on.

Lifting it up, I blink in surprise. "This is good."

"I'm the best." She winks and I nod. "You are, there's no argument about that from me. So, is this the kind of thing you do?"

The small picture she's working on looks as if it was painted by Monet, and she screws up her face and glances at it critically.

"A lot of the time it's artwork. This particular one is a copy of a copy. Two sisters grew up with it, and when their mother died, they only had the one fond memory. They couldn't agree who got to keep it, so they came here and asked for an exact replica to solve the problem. They will share the cost and take turns in hanging the original, but have the copy in place in the meantime. It's a little odd if I'm honest, but it works for them."

"How much do you charge for forging Art?"

I laugh as she shakes her head. "This one is $500. Rather

less than the original and more than the copy their mother owned. They wanted the little blemishes that have appeared over time that wouldn't show on a shop bought copy. See, this little tear in the corner and the slight yellowing around the edges."

I study the picture and feel proud of her. She's certainly talented, and I delve a little deeper.

"So, do you advertise, how do people know of your talents?"

"I have a website and an online presence. Word of mouth usually trumps everything, though."

Thinking about the reason she's in my life at all, I wonder about the person who ordered the coin. It doesn't seem a coincidence that she was used, but why someone on my doorstep?

For the first time since I met her, I start to question her involvement. What was surely just a coincidence is starting to look a little different now, and she says, "Hey, you've gone quiet on me, what's up?"

She looks interested and I sigh. "I was just wondering about why you were asked to replicate the coin. Surely, they could have used a more untraceable organization, I mean, I'm not saying anything against you but it's a little close to home, wouldn't you say?"

"I suppose, maybe it's someone local, someone who knows I'm here and thought you would never find out."

"Possibly." My mind is working overtime right now because, to be honest, I've just left this to Ryder to investigate because I've been more interested in finding Ella than the truth behind the reason she's here.

She sounds worried. "Do you think it's someone close to you, a friend maybe, a business associate, someone who works for you?"

She looks around and I share her concern. It's all a little

close to home and suddenly, I feel like the biggest fool in the world when I realize I've put us both in danger just being here.

With a firm resolve, I stare at her with genuine remorse, because she doesn't deserve to be caught up in this shit storm.

"I'm sorry, darlin', this isn't going to work."

"What isn't?"

Her eyes are wide and I see the tears building because she probably thinks I'm ending our involvement. Far from it in fact, because now more than ever I need her close.

"I'm sorry, but you need to come back to the safety of the casino. Just the fact we're here tells the person responsible we're onto them."

"But…"

"Bring what you need, I'll set you up from the apartment. Until we have the person, or people responsible, I'm not letting you out of my sight."

She makes to argue and I hold up my hand, fixing her with the usual bastard expression I use on my business associates. "Just do it because god help me, if you go against me on this, you will open up a side to me you wish you'd never seen."

She appears to shrink under the force of my anger and just sighs. "Fine, have it your way, for now, but just for the record, this picnic sucks, you suck and your whole fucking world sucks."

She looks so adorable when she's angry, I feel like ripping her clothes off right here and now but instead I take her hand.

"Come, I'll get the guys to strip the shop and set it up back at the apartment. I think the sign can go back up and we'll put a number on it for orders."

She looks so defeated I feel bad and say more gently,

"Trust me, Ella, it's for the best. Until we know who's doing this, we need to be sensible."

As I take her hand, I feel fiercely protective over my little wild flower. If anything ever happened to her because of me, I would never forgive myself.

CHAPTER 30

ELLA

I feel so frustrated. One morning is all I got, and it was enough to make me realize how much I need to work. It felt so good bringing back some normality to my life, only to have it whisked away in a heartbeat when Lucas swept in and put a stop to it. Part of me disagrees with him, I mean, I'm no threat to anyone, I haven't seen the person who made the order and couldn't identify them if I tried. I think he is wrong on this, and yet there's a part of me that loves what just happened. It gives me more time, time I want to spend with him. I'm not kidding myself it's forever, not even a month probably, but it's an intoxicating experience that I'm keen to carry on with and if that means a few more weeks out of the business, then what does it matter?

I'm quiet on the ride back to the casino and Lucas is intent on texting god only knows who for the entire journey. Is this what being with him would involve? Business most of the time with the odd moment of intimacy to feed the flames and keep me burning. And I am burning - for him. I can't douse the flames because Lucas Emiliano is nothing like I've

169

met before. He's dominant, insatiable, and so damn sexy my ovaries throb when he's nearby.

After a while, I say bluntly. "I want my phone back."

"No."

His answer is short, and he doesn't even look up from his screen.

"Why not?"

"Because I don't want anyone listening in on your conversations. It could be tapped for all we know."

"Then I want a different one."

He sighs. "Fine, I'll get you a company one. You can use that to call your family, at least I think that's why you need it."

"Maybe."

"What's that supposed to mean?"

"It means I do have a life of my own, Lucas. I have friends, people who care about what's happened to me, and they must be worried."

"Who?" He seems angry, as if he hasn't even considered I actually have a life, and so I decide to prod the beast a little out of my own anger and frustration.

"Well, I had a date fixed for when I got back."

"A date." His tone is low and even, but I hear the ominous undercurrent as he tenses beside me.

"Yes, some guy I met online; he seems nice, so we arranged to meet up."

"Is that so, what's his name?"

"Kenny." I say the first name that pops into my head and he nods. "Kenny…"

"Um, Santa."

Now he laughs. "Kenny Santa, interesting name. Maybe he has time on his hands outside of Christmas he wants to fill."

He openly laughs and I say dismissively, "Well, if I was making it up, I'd be more creative than that."

"So, Kenny Santa, what's he like, old, white beard maybe, dresses in red."

"No, actually he's tall, dark and handsome, totally ripped and an um, personal trainer. Yes, so fit he looks too good to be true."

"Obviously."

"What?"

"Too good to be true because he probably isn't - true that is."

"What's that supposed to mean?"

"Well, if he's real and let's just imagine for one moment that he is, why is he online dating? Secondly, the name seems a little weird too, I mean, Kenny Santa is just odd."

"Not as much as Lucas Emiliano."

"If you say so." He smirks and I feel like a petulant child as I shrug. "So, why is it so hard to believe that I have a date?"

"It's not, it's just I smell bullshit when I hear it. You're just pissed that I'm telling you what to do. You hate it and you hate that I'm right. You're rebelling and acting like a child because you're struggling to regain control over your life. You hate losing control to me, which tells me we need to work on that."

I stare at him in utter disbelief as he narrows his eyes and I almost see smoke coming from them. He wraps his hand around my wrist and pulls me roughly toward him and whispers, "There's somewhere I want to show you when we get back, it may make you understand your position here a bit more."

"My position." I feel a little faint as he says darkly, "I have rethought the terms of our arrangement for both our mutual benefit. You can thank me later."

"For what?"

"For making you the offer of a lifetime."

He releases me and leans back saying dismissively, "Now shut the fuck up, I need to answer this text."

I'm not sure I have enough expletives in my vocabulary to answer him satisfactorily, so instead I slump back in my seat and stare at the passing scenery with an anger that is growing by the second. How has this happened?

How have I allowed myself to be placed in this position? My life was shaping up nicely and then he entered it like a howling storm wreaking devastation on everything I had built. Now he has a plan, there's something telling me he's about to make me an offer I should refuse. I already know I'm not strong enough to refuse him anything because somehow, I have fallen in love with an enigma and until I work out how to deal with this, I'm just hanging on tight and seeing where this crazy ride takes me.

CHAPTER 31

LUCAS

I don't know why I never thought of this before. It's perfect and I'm a fool for not thinking of it earlier. I was so on edge having her stay in my apartment I forgot who I was for a moment. Ella is my Kryptonite. She is slowly destroying me inside and I need to regain control. It's who I am, what I do, and now I have the perfect answer. I get to keep her and on my terms. She will love every minute and we get an arrangement of the most delicious kind.

I'm keen to get this sorted so I wrap up my texts and as soon as the car sweeps into the underground car park, I'm pulling her from it with an urgency that surprises even me.

We ride my private elevator in silence because I am thinking my plan through. Ella appears angry, and that excites me even more. This couldn't be more perfect if I scripted it myself and so, as soon as we exit the elevator, I say darkly, "Come, I have something to show you."

She follows me in silence and I wonder what she'll make of this.

We head to the furthest corner where there are some stairs leading upward. The door that guards them is only accessed by my finger print, ensuring only I have access. Some may call it a panic room, the perfect place for a target to hide in safety. I have a more depraved function for this room and have only brought a handful of whores here before to test it out. I come here when I'm feeling at my most depraved. My darkest point and part of me is screaming at me not to bring Ella here. The thing is, somehow, I know she'll love this every bit as much as I do, and so my heart beats with excitement as I prepare to reveal the dark side to my soul.

As I open the door, the darkness greets us and she says nervously, "What is this place?"

Flicking on the lights, I just stare as the penny drops.

She looks frightened, sick even, and yet there's a spark in her eyes that tells me I was right. She's interested.

"Is this what I think it is?"

Her eyes are wide as she stares around the room in disbelief. "It is."

"But..." She's lost for words, and I push her into the room a little. "Take a look around, ask me any questions. I'm guessing you have a few."

"I'm happy that she steps inside instead of turning to run, and I watch with interest as she prowls around what is in reality a dungeon. A sex room where only the depraved play. A room no decent person should ever set eyes on and a place to purge the darkest thoughts from a sadist's mind.

There's the wooden cross on the wall with leather restraints dangling from the sides. The large bed in the center with no covers, only a wipe clean padded bench to inflict the most exquisite torture. The various toys hung on the wall that bring me the greatest pleasure. This is my playroom and I am running the risk of Ella hating me with every bone in her body.

"Wow." Her soft voice echoes around the room and she

shakes her head. "You know, I've read Fifty Shades with the rest of them and never thought things like this really existed. Do you come here often?"

She laughs softly and I laugh with her. "I come here a lot."

She giggles and my heart settles. She doesn't hate me.

"You know, Lucas, I feel a little like that woman in Fifty Shades, are you about to make me sign a contract to be your slave?"

I nod. "Something like that."

"Interesting."

"What's interesting about a contract?"

"Nothing but the interesting thing is, why you think I'd agree? I mean, I'm flattered and all, but it's not really me. To be honest, this whole experience is a little surreal. First, there was that whole Pretty Woman thing with the clothes and stuff. Now there's this, making me wonder what's next?"

"That's up to you."

"Is it, I doubt that?"

Sitting on the edge of the bed, I stare at her with interest.

"What do you want, Ella—really want?"

She appears to hesitate and her cheeks burn as she looks to the floor. I say nothing and she runs her fingers through her hair with distraction and says sadly, "I want to *live*, Lucas. I don't want to settle for the ordinary. I want to be free to make my own choices, to live my best life but I want excitement and the unusual, so maybe there's a part of this that does interest me—excite me even but I'm not sure it's really enough for me."

"Then what is?" I think I hold my breath as I wait to hear what's in her heart. She told me she loved me in one impetuous moment of madness. Is that what she wants, the hearts and flowers and declarations of love because if it is, I'm screwed because I know I can't give her that. I can give her anything else but that.

She sighs. "I want it all, Lucas, the whole package. I'm not talking about money or the lifestyle that brings with it. I'm talking about the relationship. It doesn't even have to be marriage and babies, I'm too young for that right now. I want my independence, my business, and yet I want to be in love with a man who sets me on fire with one look. Someone to share my thirst for life, someone a little edgy, who colors outside the lines and makes me feel so hard I look forward to every hour we're together. Somehow, I think you tick those boxes, Lucas, but you're holding back from me. You want me, I know that, but for how long? You like to control; I think that's pretty obvious right now, but you're afraid to let anyone in. I would always feel on the outside, just a distraction, someone to play with until you get bored and I'm not sure where that would leave me."

"It would be fun though." Even I hate myself right now as I say the first words that crawl into my thick brain. "Yes, it would be fun, but it wouldn't be enough."

She shakes herself. "Anyway, it doesn't matter what I want, it's what we have now that counts, so come on, show me what this fuck palace can do, I'm dying to find out."

She grins and looks so wicked it makes me almost come already, and I stare at her with the strangest feeling inside. Ella Quinn is an intoxicating woman, and she doesn't even realize it. She's so shady and yet so pure and innocent. She begs to be corrupted and then would probably head off and bake an apple pie to take to the priest in church on a Sunday. She is the most interesting, sexy, beautiful woman I have ever met and the one I fear losing the most. She's unlike any other woman I have ever met and would probably walk away without looking back if she wanted to. If I want to keep her, I need to prove I'm worthy and that is what I am struggling most with. I'm not. I never will be all the time I live like this.

My heart is not for the taking, it never will be, and yet I have a feeling that's the only thing that would keep her by my side.

To my surprise, she starts removing her clothes and I watch with a passion that surprises me. Just seeing her acceptance of the darkest part of my soul makes me more emotional than I ever thought possible. As she walks slowly toward me, I can't tear my eyes away and as she drops to her knees and bows her head, she gives me everything I thought I wanted.

"Is this what you had in mind, master?"

Her soft voice cuts through the layers of the hard shell I have set in place and waft around my soul. Hearing her submit to me sends me to a place I've never been before, and I'm in no hurry to leave. Removing my belt, I say darkly, "Yes, flower, this is exactly what I had in mind."

CHAPTER 32

ELLA

I don't recognize myself anymore. This place, it's so dark I should run screaming from the room. But it's Lucas. It suits him and makes me understand him a little more. I suppose I've always known he was a dominant. I see many indications of that, but then there's the other side to him I love the most. The emotional, vulnerable side that he struggles to hide. I expect he needs this in his life to reign that in and keep him grounded. I wasn't kidding when I said I want more but I know he's in no position to give me that, so while I'm here, I'm keen to experience the whole Lucas Emiliano experience package and I'm not lying, I'm looking forward to that.

My heart thumps as I keep my eyes lowered and I can feel the tension in the room. I'm aware that he removes his clothes and I feel my desire coating me below. I am so turned on right now because it's the unknown. What will he do? I trust him enough to know I'm safe, which adds to the fantasy.

He growls low in his throat. "In this room you are my slave and obey everything I say. Our language is classic traffic lights. Red for stop, amber for unsure, and green for go. Do you understand?"

"Yes, sir." I can't even believe I'm going to do this and he says ominously, "We will start off slow, test your limits."

I say nothing and wonder if this is such a good idea. It could change everything and may ruin what we have already. His voice cuts through the fog in my brain as he says firmly. "Go to the bench and lie face down. Prepare to be restrained."

I can't even look at him as I head to the bench and do as he says, before lowering myself face down onto the padded fabric that feels strangely comforting. Without a word, he binds my wrists and ankles until I am lying spreadeagled out and I hear him remove something from the wall.

"This may hurt, but it will only be for a second. Do you accept that?"

"Yes, sir." I think I hold my breath as I wait for something to hit my skin and know it's going to hurt, why wouldn't it and as I feel the sting of leather against my bare ass, I bite my lip. Another follows it and yet it's not unpleasant and as my body adjusts, I feel strangely liberated.

The fact I'm being restrained doesn't concern me. I trust Lucas, I know this is purely for pleasure and I'm keen to experience that. As I feel his soft kiss on my bare ass, I shiver a little and I prepare myself for more. The blows get more frequent. Harder and still, I say nothing. No sound at all as I test how far I can go with this. Part of me *wants* it to hurt, to feel the bite and allow my body to release those chemicals inside me that make everything go away. For so long I have had total control over my life except where it concerned my family's health. I was drowning in my inability to help make it all go away and so fearful of being alone. Now they are on the road to recovery and in a safe place, the relief has been hard to deal with. I have lived with pain and desperation for so long, I love the release this is giving me. It's as if the pain is being released into the atmosphere, and so I cry out as the tears of relief flow down my cheeks as Lucas strikes me harder each time.

I hear the concern in his voice as he says firmly, "Remember the code word, I can stop."

"Green, sir."

I am unwavering in my response because now he's started, I couldn't possibly tell him to stop. With every blow, each one harder than the last, it helps heal a pain I never knew was inside me. It's so good to feel *actual* pain, rather than the emotional baggage I have been carrying around for some time now. I never knew how pent up the emotion was, the worry about mom, Hannah, and her brush with death. The fact I have no one to turn to, nobody to ask for help. The burden of caring for them firmly at my door.

Finally, I am lying here, exposed and confined, and there is nowhere to go but face my emotions. The tears are running down my face like a dam that broke its bank and I have no way of brushing them away. No way of pretending everything is ok and no way of controlling the emotion inside me and I need this pain to make sense of the past few years which have been building to this point.

Suddenly, Lucas stops and I feel the bonds loosen and he pulls me hard against him. He cradles me like a baby as I sob in his arms and he holds my head to his chest, murmuring soft words of love. I cry in his arms like I have never cried before and don't even register how sore my ass feels. I am so grateful to him for punishing my demons from inside me, the relief is overwhelming as I lay spent in his arms, as he rocks me gently like he would a baby.

After a long time has passed, he whispers softly, "Do you want to talk about it?"

I feel like a child being consoled by an adult and far from feeling weird, it just feels normal to me.

I nod and whisper, "Thank you. I know you probably think I'm some kind of crazy mixed-up lunatic, but that was so…"

He laughs softly, "Purging?"

I nod and he says in a low voice, "I get it, Ella. Not many do, but I'm one of the lucky ones."

"In what way?"

He sighs and grips me a little tighter.

"I use sex to release my demons. The pent-up frustration, the pain inside me and the emotions I just can't deal with. This is their release and without it I would go mad."

"Do you wanna talk about it?" I laugh softly and he strokes my hair and says to my surprise, "If you'll listen, maybe it would help."

Shifting a little, I look into his eyes and see a huge amount of pain mirrored back at me. This time I reach up and stroke *his* face, and for a moment we understand one another perfectly. We are two sides of the same coin. Emotionally wanting and fucked up by life and fate. I wonder what is so bad he needs this to ground him, and I can tell it's not going to make an easy conversation.

CHAPTER 33

LUCAS

The further I went, the more she wanted. I have never seen that before. She never wavered. She took everything and wanted more, and I only stopped because she was incapable of telling me to. It concerned me because this only works when both people involved know their boundaries and I'm not sure Ella has any. I could have flogged her to death and she would thank me for it, but that's not right. Something is very wrong with Ella Quinn, and she needs me to help her deal with that.

Hell, I have the same issues myself and I suppose I have used sex as an escape from them for many years now. Bringing her here has revealed her dark side, and yet she needs to understand how to control it. She must be in pain, but you would never know it. I had to stop for her own safety because the code word was never going to fall from her lips and there's something concerning about that. So, if I can do anything for Ella, it's teaching her how to control it. To wrap up her pain in small packages to be opened with care. I know a lot about that, and I surprised myself when I offered to reveal the reason why this room is so important to me.

I'm not sure I can form the words, but now is a good time to try. So, as I hold the soft creature that is becoming the most important part of me in my arms, I revisit a memory that could destroy me in seconds.

"I told you I was adopted."

She says nothing and just strokes my chest lightly, snuggling into my arms with her head against my heart. I can't see her face, which is probably why I continue. It's as if I'm alone in the room with an angel to hear me purge my soul, and I remember back to a time where everything was good with my life.

"I had a sister; Delilah was her name. Mom and dad were so happy to have the perfect family. One boy and one girl and they we were devoted to one another. Delilah was three, and I was five. I loved my sister, though. So beautiful, like a little angel with blonde hair and blue eyes, the complete opposite of my dark hair and brown eyes. I thought she was an angel because she was so beautiful, like a little doll and I was mesmerized by her. She took after mom and dad was besotted with her."

I find myself smiling as I let the memory of them in. It's as if they are sitting here in the room with me, bringing the sunshine in, and it feels good, warm even, when usually my days are cold because they have gone.

"I never learned what my father did for work but we had money, enough to get by. Mom cared for us and we lived in a nice house in a pleasant neighborhood. There were grandparents, aunts, cousins and everything a child needs for a happy life."

It's been a while since I've thought of my extended family and I feel bad about that. I think some of them are dead now, my grandparents certainly, but I'm guessing my cousins are rattling around somewhere, I've just never bothered to look for them.

Taking a deep breath, I prepare to purge the memories and my voice breaks a little as I remember that day.

"It was Delilah's birthday. She was turning four and our parents had decided we were old enough to be trusted in a restaurant. We were so excited because it was an unusual thing to do. We dressed up smart and mom and Delilah wore matching blue dresses. They looked so beautiful I felt incredibly proud to walk in there with them. Dad and me wore smart suits, and I felt so grown up."

Ella laughs softly and squeezes me tightly, and I drop a light kiss on the top of her head. I love having her in my arms. It feels right somehow, and I don't think I've ever allowed anyone so close in my life. I knew she was special; I just didn't realize how much and it feels good having someone to talk to at last who won't judge me and expect more than I can offer.

"The restaurant was busy; it was spring break and there were many people in town. I loved it, though. The hustle and bustle of a busy place when most of the time we lived in peace in the suburbs. I loved the crowds, the voices, the music and the excited conversation and I was enjoying every second of it."

Ella kisses my chest and I stroke her hair as if petting a cat and I love the intimacy of this moment. It must hurt to sit but she doesn't say a word and as the memory returns, I stiffen a little and she whispers, "It's ok, Lucas, take your time."

Pulling back the dark curtain that hides my heart, I let the memory step out into the light and say dully, "Then it all changed. Suddenly, the noise changed from excitement to fear. I wasn't sure what was happening, but I heard gunfire like in the movies. Screaming replaced laughter and it all happened so fast I never got a chance to process what was happening. I remember Delilah's face as plain today as back then because hers was the last one I saw."

I can't face it, it's too painful and I start to shake. I can't do this.

Then a soft voice rings out, "Breathe, Lucas, take your time."

Ella grips me tightly and somehow, having her in my arms, safe in the private room with no sounds and no chance of being interrupted, calms my soul a little and I whisper, "One minute my little sister was staring at me with horror and then she was gone. Her once perfect face was destroyed in seconds as a bullet ripped through her skull followed by several more. It was like a scene from the most violent movie and I registered nothing but the sight of my sister lying face down with a huge hole where her skull used to be. I vaguely registered being pushed down to the ground, under the table with a larger body covering me. I didn't understand who it was, or what was happening because all I could see was my sister, taken from me by the devil in front of my disbelieving eyes."

I squeeze Ella so tight it must hurt, but she says nothing as I say roughly, "By the time the gunfire ceased, I was in shock. I never remembered leaving the restaurant, what happened next and what happened to everyone around me. It's only when I woke up in the hospital with a strange woman beside me that I realized I was in Hell."

I can tell Ella is crying, the moisture on my chest tells me that but you wouldn't know because there is silence in the room with only the steady beat of our hearts reminding me we're still living.

"Turns out both my parents died with Delilah that day. It always gave me comfort knowing they were together in death at least. The body that covered me was the man who since adopted me. The Casino King who was the target that day. A violent introduction to a life that has always been the same. The woman beside my bed was my new mom. A woman I loved so hard it hurt because she saved me. She loved me as if I was her flesh and blood and I owe them everything. That day fifty people lost their lives because of a business deal. A license that was refused and a deep grudge left in its place. My new parent's guards gave back as good as they got and after the gunfight, when the dust settled, it was apparent the killers were dead along with dozens of innocent people caught in the crossfire. Luckily for me, I survived, but only because my father protected me. They were at the next table and he always said it was a gut reaction to protect the innocent. Mom was being shielded by her own close protection and yet he did what was natural at the time and I will always be grateful to him for that. Because we were sitting so close to him, we never stood a chance. I was given a second one, and they took me in and raised me as theirs. They helped me through, got me professional help, and I made a life for myself from the ashes of a broken one. But as much as I loved them, I never forgot my own flesh and blood and the family I was so proud to call my own."

I shift and turn Ella's face to mine and impulsively kiss her lips softly. Maybe I need the physical contact, the reassurance she is still here, but it's suddenly important to connect with her. Her arms wrap around me and she kisses me back fiercely and yet this is not sexual. It's a loving gesture that settles my heart, showing me I'm not alone right now. She understands and is with me on this purging journey.

After a while, I pull back and bury my face in her hair and as the tears fall into it, I feel a freedom I can't explain. I voiced my darkest thoughts and now they're out in the open it's not so bad. I haven't died, I'm still here, but it changes nothing except making me feel cleansed somehow.

Then I sigh and say roughly, "So, you see, Ella, how can I bring someone close—ever? The target may have changed, but I will always be one. It's the nature of the job I do and yes, I surround myself with protection, but so did my family. Having lost every important person in my life, how can I offer up another only to be taken from me? I can't do it, so I surround myself with people who don't matter to me. I don't let anyone in and I don't give anything back but material things. No attachment, no pain. It has to be this way, which is why I am offering you a different kind of relationship. I get to keep you, but I don't love you. Nobody will know how much you mean to me, and I will show you how I feel in a depraved way. That is why I brought you here, that is why I want you to understand why I can never love you, marry you, make a life with you because if anything ever happened to you, I wouldn't survive."

For a moment we sit in silence as I lay my heart on the line. She has to understand in order for her to accept me for who I am. I know we are the same, we love too much. Her love for her family is slowly destroying her, she has taken on the burden of responsibility and is afraid of losing them, of being alone. I can help her with that, but not at the cost of my own heart. I love her, I know I do, but I won't ever tell her that.

She needs freedom, she told me, and yet my love is a prison. A gilded prison that stifles, suffocates and will end in heartache. Ella is a wild flower that needs the sunlight to thrive. I can only offer her darkness, which is why it needs to be this way, or not at all.

CHAPTER 34

ELLA

*L*ucas has broken me all over again. His story is so devastating, and now I know why he is the way he is. I'm not sure I understand it, but I have to accept it.

As we walk from the room, it's with a new understanding. For now, we have each other. A kind of fucked up relationship that only two lost souls can be in. Both of us protecting our hearts from what life can throw at them and doing it with the best intentions but all the wrong reasons.

Lucas made love to me as soon as we returned to his bedroom. I'm in no doubt about that. It wasn't sex. It was gentle, loving and filled with emotion. He treated me like the finest porcelain china and despite the raw burn on my ass, he calmed the pain by driving me to ecstasy over and over again.

We left our conversation in that room and I know it's a place that will become familiar to us. There we can unleash the parts of us we don't want exposed in the light. A place to heal and bleed the pain. Relieve the pressure with a like-minded soul. I will submit to his wishes in that room, but nowhere else. It will be a game, a way of life and a destiny, but it will be temporary. I know that now because I need to protect my heart and if Lucas won't give me his, then I need to walk away—just not yet. One baby step at a time, that's how it will be because I can't bear the thought of that day ever happening. I need him to drive that change because the thought of breaking his heart doesn't sit well with me.

The next few days are ones of adjustment. True to his word, Lucas moves my business into a room in his cavernous apartment. While he works, I work with only Tom for company when he brings me meals and Lucas when he returns from work looking as if the world is about to end. I know he's worried, something in his business is not going well, but he never speaks of it and I don't ask. We use each other to escape to a happy place and only the conversations I have with mom and Hannah keep me grounded and remind me of normal life outside the gold-lined bubble I'm sitting in.

I don't tell them of Lucas, just that I've met someone and we're having fun. Nothing more, no deep love, just fun. Just telling them that feels wrong. As if I'm denying him somehow, but I'm building a shell around my heart for my own self-protection.

The phone rings as I'm finishing up and my heart lifts when I see Hannah's name flashing on the phone that Lucas arranged for me.

"Hey, how are things?"

"All's well. I had a check-up yesterday, and the doctor is pleased with my progress."

"That's so good, honey, you're doing so well."

I always feel relief accompany her words because I live in fear of a different voice on the end of that line and a different conversation replacing it as they tell me Hannah's heart never survived.

"So, Ella, I was wondering..."

"**What?**" I smile into the phone because Hannah sounds so happy, it's infectious.

"Well, Evan wants to take me to a cabin in the mountains to recuperate now I can travel. It would be so good if you could come too. Maybe we could catch up, you know, spend some time together."

I feel a little surprised and say carefully, "**That's not much fun for Evan, I'm sure he wanted you to himself.**"

There's an awkward pause and then she says quickly, *"Well, he would, um, have Harvey to go fishing with and do men's things."*

"**Harvey who?**"

My heart sinks as I sense I'm being set up and Hannah laughs nervously.

"Look, hear me out. Harvey is a really nice guy. He's a dentist, so great potential. He met Evan at high school and they've been friends ever since. Now, I know he's not your usual type, a good solid person with a respectable job, but quite honestly, you could do a lot worse than him and someone like you would bring him out of his shell a little. I know you would be good together, so what do you say, a few days away with me and potentially the man of your future?"

I feel so conflicted. How can I go, how can I not go? I want to see my sister; I need to see her and it would be good to spend a few days with her, but this Harvey sounds dull as anything. I can already tell that by the tone of Hannah's voice.

"**But, Hannah, I told you I'm kind of seeing someone.**"

"Yes, but you also said it wasn't serious. Come on, honey, live a little, take a bit of time out to meet someone your sister approves of. I know you and this guy is probably a heartbreaker. Some flash guy who has turned your head and promised you the world, only to break it off and do the same to someone else a few weeks from now."

The most annoying thing about having a sister is that she knows me so well and I know she's right. Lucas *is* that guy, but I'm not done with him yet and that's why I can't possibly go with her.

Deciding to let her down gently, I say evenly, **"I'll think about it, no promises, mind."**

She squeals so hard, I hold the phone away from my ear and I laugh softly.

"Anyway, I should go." I hear a door slam and she says quickly, *"That's Evan I'll tell him the good news."*

She hangs up before I can object and as I cut the call, I hear "What will you think about?"

Lucas is leaning on the door jamb watching me and I laugh self-consciously.

"Hannah wants me to join her and Evan on a mountain break."

"When?"

"She didn't say but I'm not going."

"Why not?" His words don't match the relief on his face and I laugh lightly, "Because they plan on setting me up with a friend of Evans."

"Then you're right."

"What about?"

"You're not going." Lucas looks pissed and part of me loves that, but there's the other part of me that's annoyed.

"If I want to, I'll go."

I feel my eyes flash as I grip on tight to my freedom of choice, and he scowls. "Do you want to go, with *him*?" He spits the word and I shrug. "He might be nice."

"You don't want nice."

"Maybe I do. Maybe I long for a bit of nice in my life. Perhaps this is all getting old, and the excitement is wearing off."

I face him with a battle cry and his eyes glitter with

danger as he prowls toward me. "You don't want nice, you never have. If you wanted *nice,* you wouldn't be here now."

"You speak as if I have a choice."

He laughs. "You don't."

Stopping before me, he pulls me roughly into his arms and growls, "If you want nice and if you want a safe life with a man who will bore you to sleep every evening after giving you unemotional sex, then go ahead, make the arrangements. If you want a man who excites you, tears down your principles and carves his name into them, then strip naked and kneel."

Despite myself, I laugh and he says ominously, "Are you laughing at me, flower?"

"Sorry, you make it impossible not to."

Growling, he leans down and nips on my neck hard and I squeal. "Stop."

He does it again and I feel myself rise to the challenge as I groan. "You don't play fair."

He laughs against my neck and says roughly, "Maybe we need an evening in the playroom to remind you who owns you."

Just the thought of it is enough to make me shed my clothes in seconds because that is fast becoming my favorite place to be and so I fold yet again and bend to his will.

"Yes, I think that's what's needed."

I feel the relief rather than see it and as he holds me hard against him, my heart fills with love for the complicated man who guards his heart so well.

"First we eat, then we play." He growls darkly and as if on cue, we hear the elevator ping and Lucas pulls back reluctantly. "Come, I'm hungry and you will need the energy it gives you while I remind you where you belong."

As we head to the dining room, my heart is full but that voice in my head that never goes away, reminds me what a fool I am. It's inevitable we'll walk away from each other—the clock is ticking but neither of us is prepared to face that. Maybe a trip away is just what's needed. A reminder of normality and even Harvey may play a part in making up my mind whether I come back at all.

CHAPTER 35

LUCAS

*T*om has surpassed himself tonight and arranged a meal fit for a king and his queen. I'm in no doubt at all that my queen is Ella. When she spoke about leaving and spending time with another man, it enraged me. Just the thought of it has me imagining chaining her to the cross in my playroom and keeping her there forever. I can't keep her and I can't let her go free. I need her; she needs me, and this is a fucked-up situation with no resolution. I wasn't kidding when I told her I would never love her but I lied. I already do. It's that what's scaring me the most. If I love, I lose. It will always be that way because she will be an attractive target for all the fuckers who want to get back at me. Just seeing Damian Reed demonstrate that fact when he cast his eyes on her told me as much. I know how it works and no one must ever know how valuable she is to me.

But then again, the thought of her in another man's arms, bearing his children and living a dull life in the suburbs, makes my heart bleed even more. Could this work, I'm holding onto a shred of hope that it can, but I must tread carefully and test the water first because the last thing I want is for Ella to drown in my mistakes.

As we eat, Ella chatters nonsense, which is fine by me. She always does this. Fills in the awkward silences with meaningless conversation. The weather, the color of the fucking curtains, Tom this, Tom that and funny stories she's heard on the tv. It's what I love. The sense of normality that greets me when I drag myself out from behind my desk. A loving smile and a sense of having someone close who genuinely looks forward to seeing me every day.

Then there are the nights. The endless sex and explorations of a fucked-up mind. The hours spent in the playroom while I drive Ella to destruction. She is a willing student and brings me great pleasure, and I can't remember a time when I was this happy—because of her.

After a while, I groan and she looks up in surprise. "What's up?"

"I forgot, it's Penelope's stupid brunch tomorrow. We have to go."

Ella stills and says tightly, "Penelope?"

I love the surge of jealousy in her eyes and I smile. "Adam's wife."

She visibly relaxes and I feel like the cocky bastard I am because she may pretend to be casual about things, but there's a jealous streak in my flower that I love seeing. Sometimes I prod her just to see it emerge because I love how possessive she is over me, as I am her.

"What's it about?"

"Adam told me she's keen to elevate herself as the queen of all she surveys. Having me as guest of honor would do that in a heartbeat."

"You're a little sure of yourself. Honestly, Lucas, could your ego get any bigger?"

She shakes her head as I smirk. "Just stating the facts, darlin'. Your… well, I'm in great demand around here."

"My what, Lucas?" She smirks and I sigh inside as she noticed my small slip up.

"Your master." I grin and she laughs.

"Keep telling yourself that, we both know it's the other way around."

"I'll remind you of that later when you're bound before me and I'm fucking your smart mouth."

Her eyes light up and we share a dark and twisted grin. Yes, two halves of the same coin, which is ironic really when it's that that brought her to me in the first place.

"Do I have to go?" She looks bored already, which is what I love about her. She's not interested in cosying up to the social elite, despite having the man on her arm they all want. Most women would pay to go with me, be the envy of everyone around here, but not Ella. She would prefer to be working in her new office, creating works of Art to sell to her appreciative customers.

Thinking of her gratitude in our playroom turns me on so much I'm impatient to get there and I say roughly. "Of course you have to come. Do you really think I want to be unleashed on a pack of ravenous bitches? I need you to keep them away and protect me."

She just sighs and nods. "Ok, but you'll owe me—big time."

"I can do big." I rub my crotch and she laughs. "I'll think of something else you can do to repay me, just don't expect me to enjoy meeting those people, I can't think of anything worse to be honest."

"Neither can I." We share an anguished look, and she laughs as Tom heads into the room and beams. "Have you finished; can I fetch you anything else?"

"No thanks." We both speak at the same time and Tom

smiles and then looks down. I know my staff love Ella and want us to make things work. They probably think we are— making it work and I suppose to an extent we are. We just don't have a label on it and sometimes I wonder if we're destined to drift along the way we are, both of us ignoring the fact that one can't live without the other.

As soon as Tom leaves, I say darkly, "Are you ready to accept your punishment, my little flower?"

Her eyes light up and she licks her lips, making me instantly hard.

"Then come, I'm feeling particularly devilish tonight."

As she walks behind me, I feel the anticipation growing by the second as I contemplate a debauched evening doing what I love the most. Her.

CHAPTER 36

ELLA

We reach the playroom and Lucas says darkly, "Remove your clothes and kneel."

I do as he says quickly and carefully, making sure to fold them neatly as he insists on.

Then I kneel in the corner with my head lowered and try to get my breathing under control. I think about this all day long. Anticipating the pleasure he will bring, to the point it's all I can think of. How did my life become so dark? I let him do things to me no sane woman would surely ever agree to. The trouble is, I love it. He corrupts my mind and soul, and I love every second of it. He drives me to extremes and I beg for more. My pain threshold has surprised even me, and yet I want more. Always more, and as I wait for the master to begin his lesson, I almost pant with expectation.

He approaches and I hold my breath as he slides a blindfold around my eyes and says darkly, "Stand."

I allow him to lead me across the room and as my back hits the wood of the cross, my heart leaps. Finally.

So far, Lucas had refused to chain me to the cross, despite me constantly asking to experience it. He told me I wasn't ready, I had to learn to control the pain and not let it consume me. I've tried so hard and always told him to stop when I reach that point of no return, when my mind is no longer connected to my body and allows him to inflict more pain than is right for me. So many times, I've nursed the wounds of a rough night in here when I refused to tell him to stop. The open wounds, the scars, are reminders of not being in control. Lucas is teaching me to understand my limitations, and I have been keen to learn. Now I have obviously passed the test because this is my prize.

As he binds my wrists and ankles to the cross, I shiver with expectation. He pulls the binding hard and I yelp a little and love the delicious heat it creates as it travels down my body. He leans in and gently nips my breasts and I love how turned on I am. As he moves lower and tastes my arousal, I start to pant and then as he steps back, I am delirious with anticipation when I hear the crack of the whip in the air.

"Five strokes, that's all you get."

I nod and whisper, "Thank you, master."

I feel on edge as I wait for the first one to strike, and as I hear the whoosh of air, I wait for the delicious pain to hit. He strikes me across my right breast and I cry out. It stings and hurts so much, I almost come on the spot. "Color, flower."

"Green, sir."

The next blow strikes me on the abdomen and I scream as I feel the burn before a rush of endorphins push the pain away. The next three come in rapid succession and I scream so hard I think the soundproofing is ruptured and as I slump against the cross, the tears drench the blindfold. I feel so liberated by pain words can't explain how much it means to me and as Lucas enters my body in one hard thrust, ruthlessly, punishingly and making me bang against the wooden surface, I climax so damn hard I think I pass out for a second.

His roar of release drowns out my own and as his seed

trickles down my leg, I begin to sob with tears of ecstasy. I need this so badly, I need *him* so badly, and as he unfastens my bonds and swings me into his arms, I collapse against his body with exhaustion.

We lie close together on the bed and Lucas cradles me and makes love to me, slowly, gently and with so much feeling, it crushes me all over again. The calm after the storm, the smoothing away of the pain, is every bit as desirable as the onslaught before. Highs and lows, good and evil, love and hate, all mix together into the most delicious cocktail.

Most nights we never make it back to our bed because this is where we connect the most. This is our place where we are two tainted souls finding ourselves and making sense of the world. If I could stay here with him forever, I would die happy, but life gets in the way and somewhere in the early hours, we head back to bed to get some sleep for what is sure to be an extremely testing brunch date.

"I AM REALLY DREADING THIS."

I sit in the back of Lucas's chauffeur-driven car and stare sulkily out at the landscape flashing past. Even when Lucas runs his hand up my leg and under my yellow silk dress, I don't react because I would much rather be playing at home than in a car racing toward purgatory.

His low chuckle annoys me and I snap, "What?"

"I love it when you're angry. It turns me on."

He leans over and releases my seat belt and pulls me onto his lap, lifting my dress above my waist so I grind on his crotch. With a wicked smile, he parts my panties and frees his cock and as he slides inside, I gasp with the purest pleasure.

"You're a wicked man, Lucas Emiliano, I'm going to be so uncomfortable now."

As he thrusts inside, my breathing changes and he growls, "I want you to feel me every second you're there. Feel the sticky seed inside your panties knowing I own you."

I groan and bite my lip as he thrusts harder and as I come hard on his cock; he places his hand over my mouth to absorb my screams.

Just like that, my sour mood vanishes and I giggle against his neck as my irritation passes.

"Better?" He whispers against my neck and I snuggle into him.

"Yes—thank you, although I'm guessing I smell like a whore's bed right now, you're a wicked man, Lucas."

"I never pretended to be anything else."

He nuzzles against my neck, and I love every minute of this. Being here with him, the unexpected, never knowing what he'll do next—usually involving sex. I've never felt so alive and just thinking of living a different life without him, is not a pleasant thought and as if he reads my mind, he whispers, "Don't go."

"Where?"

Thinking he's referring to the break with Hannah and god forbid Harvey, he says sadly, "Home, away with your sister, in fact, anywhere but by my side."

I shift back and stare into his troubled eyes, and my heart lurches. "But how, you said yourself you can't offer me anything outside this? That I wouldn't be safe with you and become a target, what's changed?"

Suddenly, the car comes to a swift stop and I fall against him and he sighs. "We'll talk about it later. Let's get cleaned up and deal with this shit show then we'll talk—really talk."

Dropping a soft kiss on my lips, he smiles. "Come on, did anyone tell you, you stink like a whore's bed?"

Rolling my eyes, I shift back and reach for a bunch of tissues from a box nearby and hand him a few, whispering, "I smell of you and it's the sweetest smell in the world."

This time I drop a light kiss on his lips and sigh with pleasure. I already know I can't deny him a thing, and if I'm going anywhere, it's with him by my side.

CHAPTER 37

LUCAS

I'm not sure what's happened to me, but since Ella came into my life, everything's changed and now I can't let her walk away.

This brunch is getting in the way of the rest of my life because I'm keen to have a discussion with Ella that will change everything and that terrifies the shit out of me. I'm not a man who wears his heart on his sleeve, I don't do feelings and shit, but I've changed and it's down to her. Ella Quinn was always the woman who would drive change, I think I knew that the moment she stared at me through those beautiful eyes the day we kidnapped her.

We will figure it out. We have to because when I heard she may be leaving to go on a trip with her sister and some douchebag she's never met; I was irrationally angry. Over my dead body is she spending time with another man and so I need to do anything it takes to keep her and if that's on her terms, then I'll have to accept them.

Somehow, we make ourselves respectable and Jason my driver knows better than to open that door until I give him the signal. So, almost as soon as I knock on the glass separating us from him, he opens the door and I grab Ella's hand. "Come on, honey, I'll try to make this short and sweet."

She sighs heavily and as she steps into the sunshine in her pretty yellow dress, my heart fills with emotion. Squeezing her hand hard, I feel so proud to walk beside her. She's beautiful in every way that counts and is like a breath of air, like a summer breeze as she smiles into my eyes. "Come on, how bad can it be? I'm guessing you're overreacting as usual."

Rolling my eyes, I growl, "I'll remind you of that when this is over."

Adam and Penelope live in a colonial-style house on the best street in Vegas. Huge houses dominate a pleasant district, and Adam has obviously spent a shed load of money on keeping his bride happy. Beautiful lawns and manicured perfection greet us as we head toward the large front door, flanked either side by huge trees that are adorned in lights that I'm sure transform the façade in the dusk. As if by magic the door opens as we approach and I see Adam looking resigned to what we shall receive, holding the hand of his elegant wife Penelope.

She is an attractive woman, that's undeniable, but I always found her a little aloof, cool and unemotional. She is certainly beautiful and would make a good politician's wife. Elegant, well connected and extremely polite, outlined with a hard defining edge that emphasizes her character in a bold line.

"Lucas, how lovely to see you."

She swoops in and kisses me on both cheeks, and I smell the scent of a woman who is trying a little too hard.

"Penelope, you are looking good as always."

I return the greeting and she smiles. "You always were a charmer; I can't imagine why you are still single."

"He isn't."

Ella reminds me why I love her as she interrupts, drawing

Penelope's gaze to her with a sharpness that surprises me a little.

"Oh, forgive me." Penelope turns her attention to Ella and her gaze runs the length of her as she blatantly checks her out. Ella just stands her ground and smiles. "Thank you for inviting *us*."

She emphasizes the 'us' and Adam laughs, moving in to kiss her on both cheeks and then shakes my hand.

"Penelope, this is Ella, remember, I told you she was coming."

Penelope nods. "I thought you said she was his assistant, obviously you got that wrong as well, darling."

I feel a prickle of irritation on Adam's behalf as she snaps at him and he sighs. "We should fetch our guests a drink, darling, they must be in need of one, I know I am."

He winks and Penelope apparently remembers her hostess duties and smiles. "Of course, please, let me introduce you to the crowd, Lucas. Adam, maybe you could make sure, um, Ella, wasn't it, has a drink?"

She hooks her arm through mine and makes to propel me into the room like a prize and Adam throws me an apologetic look, which is nothing like the one Ella throws Penelope. It makes me smile as they follow us through into a large open plan space that leads through to a vast garden where a pool glitters like a jewel outside.

My heart sinks when I see that half of Vegas apparently required an invitation and I am soon lost in a sea of ambitious bitches as Penelope introduces me to just about every available woman in Vegas and even some that are not.

I lose sight of Ella almost immediately and feel bad about that. She must be hating every second of this, and as I make all the right noises and smile when required, I decide to do everything I can to move this on so I can get the hell out of here.

CHAPTER 38

ELLA

*A*dam seems to be in purgatory and says with a groan, "I'm sorry, Ella."

"It's fine, Lucas is a big boy and he can look after himself. You have a lovely home by the way."

"Thank you."

He smiles, and it strikes me how handsome Adam is. I'm sure that the two of them could have anything they want in life, and I'm surprised he settled down with Penelope.

As he hands me a glass of champagne, I say with interest, "Lucas tells me you've been married for six months, you must be very happy how things turned out."

"I am." He smiles but I can tell he's lying because if that's the look marriage gives you, I'm staying single—forever.

We stand on the edge of the group crowding around Lucas and Adam sighs. "He must be hating every minute of this. Penelope promised she wouldn't throw him to the dogs and she did it as soon as he arrived."

I laugh to myself when I catch sight of his anguished expression as a bottle blonde lays her hand on his arm and gazes up at him adoringly.

"Why is she so keen to show him off like that? Surely, she doesn't need anything more than what she has already. I mean, you have it all, Adam, if you don't mind me saying so. The house, the lifestyle, contacts and surely that's enough to ensure your status among this crowd."

He smiles, but I'm surprised to see the bitterness in his eyes. "But it's not enough—for Penelope, that is, and I'm kidding myself if I think it is. You see, I never saw it before we married, but Penelope is a power-hungry wannabee. She engineers situations that make her powerful and has been begging me to set this one up for months.

"But why?"

"Because Lucas is the most eligible bachelor probably in the world right now and these women would do anything to land the prize. Sometimes I think that's the reason Penelope married me in the first place, to secure her position in his social group, ensure she's always here by default rather than marriage."

"That's kind of sad." I shake my head and he nods.

"You're telling me. Then again, I'm used to it and I have been for some time. Lucas and me, well, we're like brothers. We've always worked hard and partied harder, and it was always him. The one the woman wanted, and I was the consolation prize. It bothered me at first, but I soon shrugged it off and enjoyed the benefits it brought me."

"But you're an attractive man, you could have your pick whether you're by Lucas's side or not. Don't put yourself down."

"I can see why Lucas likes you so much, Ella, you are very complimentary."

"Only when it's deserved." I take a sip of champagne and watch the circus in front of my eyes.

"Maybe we should rescue him." Adam sounds concerned and I giggle. "No, let's make him suffer, he's got to learn how to deal with hostile situations. After all, he has life spoon fed to him most of the time. It will do him good to feel a little pain from time to time."

"Yes, well, from what I remember, he prefers to dish out pain rather than receive it. He must be in hell right now."

Wondering if Adam knows about the pain Lucas loves to give me, makes me feel a little hot and I clear my throat. "Anyway, can you point me in the direction of the rest room? I really should freshen up."

The heat and the fact that Lucas has made quite a mess in my underwear makes me anxious to clean up and Adam nods. "Of course, let me show you the way."

As we head inside, I take in all the details of a place that has been designed by the best. It's certainly impressive with its marble floor and elegant regency furniture. It looks a little ostentatious and not really homey and I say politely, "You have a lovely home."

Adam groans. "Not really, it may look like it is, but it's hardly a home, more like a showpiece."

"Don't you like it then?"

"I prefer my apartment at the casino, it's more my style."

"So, you don't actually live here then?"

"Penelope does." I stare at him in shock and he shrugs. "I work so hard to pay for this lifestyle it made sense to stay at my apartment during the week and return here on week-ends. Sometimes, Penelope comes to stay with me during the week but more often organizes her social calendar around me working. That's why occasions like this are special, it's what we do as a couple and so because I neglect her most of the time, I'm keen to indulge her a little when I am here."

"But you are newlyweds, surely any time apart is hell."

"Not really." Adam looks a little sad and I know immediately he's regretting his marriage. There's no love here and I feel sad for him. Maybe this is what the rich do, marry for position, a place in society that ticks all the boxes. Maybe I'm kidding myself that I will fit in with this world, I'm a nobody, after all. Lucas could marry the best, the one who would be accepted and belong in his world. Suddenly, I feel sick as I think about how much I'm refusing to see the truth. I'm kidding myself if I think this will ever work and Adam has inadvertently reminded me of something I think has always been at the back of my mind—I'm just not good enough and I never will be.

HE LEAVES me to freshen up and as I step inside a beautiful bathroom, I look at the slightly disheveled woman staring back at me through the mirror. Who is this girl? She's a nobody; a copycat pretending she's good enough.

I have never felt so low in my life, so insignificant and as if I don't measure up. I may be dressed like the rest of them courtesy of Dixie and Tom, but I don't really fit in. Lucas may think he wants me now, but he never promised me anything other than sex and more fun that a girl can stand. He's already told me he won't ever give me his heart, and I was the fool who thought differently.

Now I see what the likes of Penelope see when they look at me. I see someone pretending she is better than she is, daring to imagine she is on an equal footing with the rest of them. I'm a fool and as the tears blind me, I decide to hide out until this is over and then when we leave, I need to consider my options because I don't want to feel like this, to feel unworthy. I'm better than that, so with a sigh, I splash some water on my face and wash away the evidence of Lucas inside my panties, feeling like some kind of cheap whore he has used for his own amusement.

One last look in the mirror reminds me what an idiot

looks like, and I head back outside to get this over with as quickly as possible.

As I close the door softly behind me, I hear, "There you are. I've been looking for you."

CHAPTER 39

ELLA

*T*urning around, my heart sinks when I see Penelope looking at me with a critical appreciation and I don't miss the slight sneer on her face, or the derision in her eyes.

"Please, Ella, allow me to show you something before we return to my guests, you may be interested in this."

I doubt it, but I feign interest and smile, although it pains me to do anything but scowl at this bitch who obviously knows she's better than me.

"That sounds interesting, of course."

We walk along her beautiful hallway and she leads me to a door at the end, saying in a low voice, "Adam told me Lucas had found someone to play with, which surprised me a little because they don't usually last the night. You must have something the rest don't."

"Excuse me." I can't believe she actually went there and voiced the thoughts in her head, and she smiles maliciously. "Then I asked myself why? What does this girl have above all others? Surely there must be something to gain such a man's interest."

I can't believe how rude she is and say tightly, "Listen, thanks for the tour but no thanks. I think I'll be heading back to Lucas now."

To my surprise, she grabs my arm roughly and hisses. "I don't think so."

She pushes me into the room and as I catch my breath, she turns and closes the door, locking it behind us. "What are you doing?"

I stare at her in shock as she laughs bitterly. "Finishing the job."

"What are you talking about?"

As I utter the words, my breath catches as I stare down the barrel of a gun that she is pointing directly at my head.

"I'm sorry about this, Ella, but we don't have long. If I know Lucas, he'll make his excuses inside of thirty minutes and leave. The trouble is, I can't let that happen, so you are my only hope."

As I stare into the eyes of a deranged woman, I feel real fear in my heart. She's mad, it's obvious, and is holding a gun that she is obviously not afraid to use.

"Why?" I whisper the words and hate that my voice shakes in fear and she shrugs. "Money, power, favors owed. Take your pick because this whole show has been put on for one reason only."

"The brunch?"

She laughs. "Not the brunch you foolish girl, the marriage, the pretense of being the perfect wife. It was all a lie, a twisted engineered façade to get me to this point, and you are the one who will take the fall. Genius really because the target has always been Lucas, and it has taken several months of planning to reach this point."

I try so hard to organize my thoughts; to get my head straight so I can work my way out of this horror show, but she doesn't give me time and snarls, "To be honest, I can't wait to get this done. Waiting for the opportunity has been so tedious, and if I have to endure one more night of Adam, I'm liable to finish him off."

"Why are you doing this?" I repeat my question to try to stall for some time, anything to make this go away, and she shrugs, "The money's good."

She waves to a seat facing the door and says roughly, "Sit."

I swallow hard and consider my options, which appear to be in short supply right now and so I do as she says, trying hard to get my breathing under control.

As she advances, the tears blur my vision because all I can think of is Lucas. She wants him dead, but why?

The pain in my heart is so real and raw, and I know it's not down to my own safety - it's his. This can't happen, I won't let it happen, and yet she is the one standing there with a gun to my head.

She doesn't hang around either and before I know it, she snarls, "Place your hands behind your back."

She advances quickly and I feel the cold hard steel of the barrel of the gun against my temple and have no other choice but to do as she says.

I feel her fasten something around my wrists, and then she reaches for my purse and grabs the phone from it.

"Perfect. Now I just send a text to your devoted companion and we will wait for him to arrive. This should be good."

"Please, don't hurt him, whatever you're being paid, he will pay more." I plead with her the only way I know how, and she laughs.

"I doubt that."

She starts tapping into the phone and I look around wildly for anything that could help free me from this situation. I need to think, to help Lucas because this woman is mad, I really believe that.

She throws the phone on the table beside the chair and says, almost as if she's talking about the weather, "There, that should do it. Now all we need is for him to come running and then bang, Lucas is no more. It's a shame you'll go to hell with him. The evidence will show you pulled the trigger and then turned it on yourself. Perfect and I get to be the first on the scene, the shocked hostess who stumbled upon a murder scene."

The tears blind me as I feel so helpless and as she paces the room, I pray to god Lucas never reads that text.

CHAPTER 40

LUCAS

*T*hank God for Adam. He always did have my back and I am so grateful when he pulls me away from the frenzied women who clamor around me, desperate to grab my attention.

He guides me toward the house and whispers, "I'm sorry, Lucas, I should have been more insistent when Penelope insisted you come."

"It's fine, but if you don't mind, I think I'll grab Ella and go. Where is she by the way?"

It feels wrong not having her by my side, and I'm anxious about that. The entire time those women fussed around me, I could only think of her. It's as if I need to know she's by my side to survive. She provides the oxygen allowing me to breathe and as I look around, I feel anxious that she isn't in my sight.

We reach the house and Adam says in a low voice, "There's something I need to say."

He sounds terrible, and I can tell I'm not going to like this conversation.

He directs me to his den and as I take a seat on the couch

by the fireplace, I watch as he pours us both a shot of whiskey from the decanter on the side.

"Here, I need this even if you don't."

I can see his hand shaking and my senses tell me something bad has happened and I'm desperate to find out what because Adam doesn't lose his cool. He thrives under pressure and I trust him with my business as well as having my back, so I growl, "Spit it out, Adam, you're freaking me out right now."

He looks at me through tortured eyes and says in a broken voice, "It's Penelope."

"What about her?"

I can't imagine what he's about to say and he says roughly, "I think she's having an affair."

To be honest I'm not surprised, it's classic but so soon in their marriage, that really is fast work.

"Who with?"

He sighs, "I'm not sure, but I found a phone in her purse when I was looking for my keys and I didn't recognize it. It was a slim iPhone and my first thought was she had the wrong purse. I checked, and it was locked."

"Did you manage to find the code?"

"I did, she used the same one she always uses, so I knew it was hers because of that alone."

"Not very smart, unless…"

"Unless she wanted me to find it." Adam sighs. "That was my first thought too. I checked the messages and there was only one caller. The texts were cryptic but told me she was involved in something and it was a secret. They spoke of meeting up when she gets to New York."

"I see." I feel so bad for Adam, but wonder if he's just misread the situation.

"Why do you think she's cheating on you?"

Adam looks sick as he says bitterly, "Because of the nature

of the texts. She told this person she couldn't wait to be rid of me. That I make her flesh creep and her acting skills were deserting her. She couldn't wait to be under a real man again and it was time to move things on."

My heart breaks for my friend because he wears the look of a man destroyed.

"Do you know who he is?"

He shakes his head. "I tried to trace the number, but it came up unidentified. I looked through every record we have for any mention of New York, but there was none. I played detective with my own wife and I hated every minute of it, but I obviously suck because all I have is this phone."

I exhale sharply and feel bad for my friend. I'm not surprised though, Adam rushed into things with Penelope and a fool could see she was aloof, cold even and nothing like a newlywed in love with her husband.

"So, what are you gonna do now?"

"End it. Send her packing and hope I never see the bitch again."

"Do you think she was after your money, that could be a problem?"

Adam looks so defeated it makes my blood boil and then he looks at me sadly. "No, I had her sign a prenup—luckily. No, I think the real reason she came to Vegas, to marry me, was to get close to you."

"Me!" I stare at him in surprise because if that was her intention, she failed, and he laughs bitterly. "For some reason you were our only topic of conversation. She wanted to know everything about the business, your personal life and even your favorite fucking color."

"And you didn't think that was strange?" I shake my head and he slumps back in his seat. "Not really, you're always a fascinating subject for any lady. I've kind of got used to being the barrier that prevents them getting to you, and I've made a career out of it. The fact I get laid so much is probably down to it and I used to thank you for that."

My heart goes out to my friend and I remember the bitterness in his eyes when I catch him looking sometimes. Then I remember the coin, the confusion over it, and the fact my business is going down shit creek and something clicks inside me. "Do you think she's after information for someone else? Maybe she's not having an affair, perhaps she's working for someone who is trying to bring me down. It would explain a lot."

"Possibly, but who? You have everything sewn up water-tight and only a fool would try to cast shade on your business. What would they achieve because you run things in this world? You're the man the government listens to, for fuck's sake they will only award a gaming license if you've signed it off first. It's why they come to you; why they kiss your ass to get what they want, so you recommend their business to the men in power. What kind of fool would go against that?"

His words hit me like machine gun fire, every one of them finding their mark. The picture starts to piece together before my eyes and I can't believe I haven't thought of it before—first Ryder and now me. There can only be one man responsible.

As my brain works hard processing this new information, my phone buzzes and the relief is enormous when I see the text from Ella.

Hey babe. I'm lonely without you. Just so you know, I'm waiting for you behind a door with a lock and guess what, I'm not wearing any panties. If you want to live on the wild side, come and get me. End of the hallway, last door. Knock three times and I'll show you why you keep me around.

I stare at the text in surprise. This doesn't sound like Ella at all, yet it's her phone. Something holds me back and Adam says with curiosity, "What is it, Lucas? Is it something I should know about?"

"I'm not sure, something's not right though."

Rather than head outside, I lift my phone and as soon as the person picks up, I say in a cool voice, "Did you get that?"

As he answers, my blood runs cold and his voice sounds as if it's coming from another planet.

This can't be happening, not again, and my hand instinctively reaches for my gun as the clock on the wall counts down to something that will potentially destroy me. It feels like forever, a million hours pass and then as Adam says more urgently, "What is it, Lucas, you're scaring me."

Before the last word even registers, a shot rings out, closely followed by another one.

CHAPTER 41

ELLA

I never really understood the term, 'living a nightmare' but I do now. Time has slowed and yet is passing way too fast. Nothing seems real anymore, and it's as if I'm watching events unfold through an observer's eyes. Penelope is pacing, obviously excited about something no sane person would ever imagine. She seems on edge and who can blame her, she's about to commit murder twice and already thinks she's got away with it? They say a person's life flashes before their eyes when they're about to die. I don't share that experience, which gives me hope.

I level my voice and say evenly, "Why are you doing this, surely I deserve to know the reason behind my death?"

I feel her watching me with interest and she laughs bitterly. "You deserve nothing, but I'll tell you, anyway. You are just a pawn in a far bigger game. A disposable by product of a costly war. Lucas needs to be taken out, and this is the perfect way. Nobody has ever been able to get close to him before. His team are tight and Adam was my only hope."

She laughs wickedly. "He was the easy part. Seduce Adam, get him to marry me and infiltrate Lucas's inner sanctum.

Lure him here and finish him off. Walk away because the trauma was too much and effectively ended my marriage and then live in luxury for the rest of my life with the proceeds of my crime."

"Who wants him dead?" I already know she's a pawn in this game herself, and she shrugs. "As if I know. When you play with the big boys, there are many layers to the intrigue. A spider spins her web in a very intricate way, and the reasons why are not always obvious. I have been told what I need to know and nothing more, so if you think I'm going to spill some great master plan to a girl like you—you're mistaken. You're just not important enough, and neither am I as it happens. My instructions have been relayed electronically and news flash, I don't know the person behind them."

"Then how do you know they will spare you too? You might not be paid and may not even make it to enjoy your new life."

She falls silent, which gives me hope because if I can cast doubt on this, she might not see this through and it may just end up saving our lives.

I press on. "Maybe you are just as disposable as me. We are, as you say, just pawns in a bigger game. If you do what they say, you are treading a path that could end for us all. If you think about it, they sound like someone who doesn't like loose ends. If this is what I think it is, there are already two people dead who brought me into this mess. Maybe they got caught up in something they didn't fully understand and paid the price."

"What are you talking about?"

I take a deep breath because I am about to tell her something I'm not even sure is my information to pass on, but she needs to have all the facts and it may just cast enough doubt in her mind to save us all.

"I'm here because I was hired, much like you were, to do a

job. I never saw the person, I never spoke to them and just carried out their wishes."

She looks at me sharply and I press on, conscious I don't have long.

"The person who collected the order was a beautiful young woman. She took the package and when Lucas came calling, it was to find out who my customer was because that woman was dead and so was the man she delivered it to."

Penelope looks up sharply and I see the doubt in her eyes. "So, you see, Penelope, this game is bigger than both of us. I'm in danger and so are you. If you think this ends here, you're mistaken. You will always be looking over your shoulder, wondering if they've come to finish you off, to keep you from exposing them to their enemies. You are a loose end that will need tying up, so I beg you, don't do this. Work with us to uncover the person behind this. Save our lives and your own in the bargain."

She doesn't answer because we hear someone approaching and the tension in the room is palpable. Penelope moves quickly and stands behind me as three sharp knocks are heard on the door. I make to cry out, to warn Lucas not to come in but a fist is shoved so hard into my mouth, I choke a little and before I can catch my breath a shot rings out, closely followed by another and then all hell breaks loose.

Everything goes black. I'm covered in a liquid that coats my neck and I'm face down, my head facing my knees with something heavy on my back. I hear a man's voice that I recognize immediately, and my heart pounds so hard I think it will give out on me. The only thought I have right now is one of relief because that voice isn't Lucas's. It wasn't him, but what does that really mean? Maybe that shot found its mark, and he's dead at my feet. Surely there should be more noise, shouting even, but it's as if a sense of calm has descended on the room as a voice says softly, "Stay down, Ella, you're ok."

I hear someone else come into the room and a voice I vaguely remember says in hushed tones, "Fucking good shot, that man is notching up quite a tally."

The other voice laughs softly. "He's earned his cut, that's for sure."

"Strong hands pull the weight from my back and as I look up, I see a concerned face staring into my eyes and he reaches out and places a finger on my lips. "Don't say a word, don't look behind you and just come with me."

I recognize the man that was standing beside Lucas the day I was kidnapped, Ryder King. His hard eyes are flashing with danger and his expression is grim making my soul shiver. There is blood on his hands and as I look down, I see it has come from me. Have I been shot and am too numb to feel? There is no time for questions as I hear a dark whisper behind me, "Charlie and Eddie are clearing the guests, we don't have long."

I make to turn around and Ryder hisses, "Eyes front. Now, come with me, you're safe now."

He reaches out and takes my hands that have been freed by the person behind me, and I already know that Penelope is dead. There is no sound other than the two men in the room, and it doesn't take a rocket scientist to know the blood on me is hers.

As I follow Ryder from the room, I catch sight of a reflection in the mirror on the wall and the horror of it will stay me forever. The beast who kidnapped me from the airport is lifting her body, but that's all that's left. Her head has been shattered, almost destroyed, and my knees start trembling as I hurl on the spot.

"Eyes forward and walk." Ryder's voice is firm and offers no argument and snaps me out of the horror of the scene I just saw happening behind me. Sobbing, I stumble toward him and he catches me as I fall, sweeping me into his arms and carrying me like a baby from the room. It's all a little surreal because everything is done in almost silence. The only sound was the two shots and as we pass the door, I see a bullet hole embedded in the wood, making the tears run like blood down my face. Penelope obviously fired her gun because it's at the exact position a man's head would have been, and I wonder how Ryder managed to survive at all if he was the man through that door.

As we leave the room, I don't think what happened inside it will ever leave me and as I battle the tears that are threatening to unravel me, there is only one man I want to see.

CHAPTER 42

LUCAS

*T*wo shots fired in rapid succession and Adam says quickly, "What the fuck was that?"

He jumps up and I say roughly, "Sit down, Adam, for fuck's sake just do it."

He looks at me ashen-faced and my heart pounds so hard, I think it's going to pack up on me and his voice shakes. "Lucas, what the fuck is going on?"

"Fuck if I know but that call, it was my security telling me to stay here and don't move."

"Do you think someone's in the house, someone with payback on their mind?"

Adam looks scared shitless and I'm not far off. All I can focus on are the images in my head of a different gun fight. Different people having their lives ended that day and yet this time it's not them, it's Ella and the pain is too much, too intense and I'm struggling to breathe.

Adam whispers, "Penelope, god do you think she's ok?"

"Who gives a fuck?" I can't even think about that woman but Adam growls, "She may have betrayed me but she's still my wife. What if she…"

"Adam I…"

My voice shakes as I struggle to think rationally. How can I comfort him when my life could have ended outside this room? What if Ella was caught in the crossfire? I can only hope she is standing with the rest of the guests and never sent that text in the first place. It's the only hope I cling on to as we wait for the moment of madness to pass and are given the all clear.

Ryder has been monitoring my phone since the day he arrived in Vegas and has been looking into everyone around me, every phone call, every conversation and all my computer records. He would have got that text, which is why I called him first. I do nothing without his say so and from the tone of his voice, he already knew what was unfolding outside this room.

"Stay put."

Those were his words and it's agonizing to wait. I feel powerless but know I must play my part. I trust him with my life, we all do, which is why the thought of him being taken out not so long ago, is not one I ever want to face. Without Ryder and his slick operation, none of us are safe, which is why he was the first target. Obviously, I'm next but who is doing this? It doesn't make sense and so against every part of me that has feeling, I do as he says even though I want to tear this house apart to find the only person who matters to me that I am fast realizing I can't live without.

However, I have to trust him and all I can think of is that when things are out of your hands, remember whose hands they're in. Ella is in the safest hands in this world and I have to put my trust in him on that.

I tune Adam out and think about Ella. I offer a silent prayer to God to save her and if she walks through that door, to hell with my fears. She won't ever leave my side again because now I fear her not being in my life, much more than worrying for her safety if she is. I will make her safe, I will wrap her in protection and ensure that no harm ever comes to her because I love Ella Quinn. The hole in my heart that is bleeding right now out of fear for her tells me that.

Adam sounds desperate as he jumps up, "Fuck this, I'm heading outside."

I don't even think and draw my gun and say ominously, "Sit the fuck down, you're going nowhere."

He stares at me in disbelief as I hold my gun at his head and he stutters, "What the fuck, Lucas, what's happening?"

"I'm keeping us safe; you go through that door and you might not make it. This is our only chance at surviving this shit storm and if you think I'm about to lose another person who means everything to me, you're mistaken."

To my surprise, his eyes shine with tears and he nods. "Thanks, man."

At this moment it's just the two of us. Two men who stand to lose everything but have always had each other's backs. Two brothers by choice not blood, who would kill for each other and I will not let him fall if I can prevent it. I will always have Adam's back and if that involves hard decisions from time to time, then I'll make them in a heartbeat because I will *not* lose him. It would break me, so an eerie silence descends on the room as we wait for our destiny to be fulfilled and neither one of us are responsible for the outcome of that.

IT FEELS like hours but can only be a few minutes before we hear footsteps approaching and my finger curls around the trigger of my gun, as I aim it at the door.

A gruff voice outside has me lowering my weapon and as the door opens, I think every favor I have ever asked from God is repaid as Ryder heads into the room carrying a blood-soaked Ella. Jumping up, I run toward her and as Ryder lowers her to the ground, she turns to face me with a mixture of relief and fear.

Her voice breaks as she whispers, "Oh my god, Lucas, thank God."

She falls into my arms and as they wrap around her, I pull her close and whisper, "Are you hurt?"

She shakes her head and the relief hits me hard and as my eyes connect with Ryder's, I direct all my gratitude his way.

Then I hear Adam shout, "Is Penelope ok?" and I don't think there is a sound in the room as the atmosphere darkens and Ryder shakes his head. "I'm sorry."

I am so torn right now because I can't bear to let Ella leave my arms for a second but as Adam falls to his chair, I know he needs me right now but Ella beats me to it and breaks free and races across to him. "Adam, stay focused, listen to Ryder, you have to."

I stare at them both in shock as she kneels before him and takes his hands in hers. Her compassion for him tears at the already jagged shards of my heart that has been battered so cruelly in such a short time. The tears run down her face as she whispers, "If you have to grieve, remember her for the woman she was with you, not the woman she really was. Hold onto those images and treasure the good times because they are all you have left."

"What happened?" Adam's voice is rough and Ella looks at Ryder who says gruffly, "Someone fetch us all a fucking drink, you need to hear this before we leave this room."

Reaching for the decanter, I pour us all a glass of whiskey and Ella hands hers to Adam and stares at him with compassion. As our own eyes meet, the love shining from hers mends every broken piece of my heart because there's an understanding in them that tells me she feels the same. Ella is going nowhere and she knows that, so I smile and nod and love seeing the relief in her eyes.

As Ryder starts to talk, my only concern right now is for the broken man who has just lost his wife.

CHAPTER 43

ELLA

he relief is overwhelming, but I will have to park it because one look at Adam told me he is the priority right now. Lucas is safe, I am safe, but Adam is broken and once he discovers the truth, he may not recover.

It was instinctive to go to him; to help him though what will be his darkest hour because Lucas and me, we're the lucky ones. We have each other and a life that's ours for the taking if we lower our guards enough to make that happen. However, that's for another day because what happens now takes precedence over that and so I hold Adam's hand as Ryder fills him in on what happened in the room.

Lucas exhales sharply when Ryder finishes and looks at Adam with so much compassion, I struggle to breathe as he says gruffly, "I'm sorry, bro."

His voice breaks and he moves across and slings his arm around Adam's shoulders, but I'm not sure he is registering anything but the pain inside him right now.

"She's really gone."

He stares at the floor and Ryder says softly, "It was the only way, I'm sorry. She had a gun to Ella's head and was intent on shooting Lucas, ending his life for reasons we still don't know about."

"Couldn't you have disarmed her, captured her, anything but that?"

"No."

Ryder offers no apologies, no words of comfort, just the cold hard facts which Adam doesn't realize he really needs right now.

He sighs heavily and says in his no-nonsense voice, "Charlie is waiting to take you back to the Casino. Leave us to deal with things here."

I don't miss the look Lucas and Ryder share as we walk from the room. This isn't finished and from the looks of things, it's only just started.

~

We sit either side of Adam in the car. It was a strange exit from a house that was previously filled with guests and loud conversation. As we walked outside everyone had gone and there was only the discarded champagne glasses, bottles and silver trays piled with food that gave any indication anyone had been there at all. Adam has shut down; retreated to a dark place in his mind and there is no conversation, no reaction from any of us. It's as if time has stood still all around us and the ghosts of the past are waving us off to an uncertain future.

We make the ride home in silence and head to Lucas's apartment by way of his private elevator. I know we can't leave Adam; he will have many questions and needs to be among people who care and I know Lucas does, it's obvious from the emotion in his eyes as he looks at his unofficial brother with concern.

Occasionally, he looks at me and I see the emotion

breaking that is hard to deal with right now. There is a lot to say and yet nothing to say and we both know we have all the time in the world to talk and so an easy acceptance of the situation settles on us as we do our best for his best friend.

We reach the apartment and Lucas says gruffly, "Adam, you can stay here. Your room is ready and don't even think about telling me no."

Adam nods but looks so grateful it brings tears to my eyes. "Thanks man." Lucas nods and I see his throat bob as he struggles to keep his shit together. Slipping my hand in his, I say softly, "I'm going to clean up, will you be ok?"

He nods and I feel his eyes burn into my back as I leave them to it and swallow the sob that is threatening to be my undoing. I'm trying so hard to be brave, to help them through this, but I can't shake what just happened. Things like that don't happen to girls like me. I have a safe life, an ordinary life; one with no drama and certainly not murderous bitches out to end it.

Thinking of Penelope and her sticky end should make me feel compassion for a woman who was caught up in something she didn't understand. But how can I, how can I have any compassion for a woman who made her own choices even when she was questioned on them? What she has done to Adam will take years to forgive, if he ever will. He will be damaged, and I only hope he finds a way to overcome it.

I head to the shower and can't wait to feel the water wash away the evidence of a brutal slaying. Whoever pulled that trigger wasn't messing around, and I doubt Penelope even registered what happened. I hope so anyway because knowing that was your final breath would have been scary as hell, but it all happened so quickly, I doubt she even knew about it.

As I soap my body, I scrub hard to remove any trace of her from it and I don't hear the door open and the first thing

I know is when Lucas enters the shower and pulls me against him. Just feeling his strong arms holding me so tenderly is enough to unlock the floodgates and as I sob in his arms, I let the emotion have its day. He stands holding me hard against him as the water washes away the horror and nothing else matters but him, me and the fact we're alive to tell the tale.

CHAPTER 44

 ucas

I AM SO TORN. On the one hand, I need to help my friend though his darkest hour but Ella needs me and to be honest, I need her more than I realized. I can't ignore the fact my heart aches when she isn't in my arms and after what she went through today, it's instinctive to want to hold her, soothe away her worries and make everything better.

As soon as Adam went to freshen up, I was off in search of her. I just want to hold her, reassure her, and make her agree to never leave my side. Every nightmare I ever had came back to haunt me today and yet we made it, we survived, which tells me not to waste another minute of our lives. If I'm sure of anything it's that and Ella and me were destined to be together and I'm not one to go against destiny and I hope she feels the same.

After a while, we sit on the bed wrapped in robes and just hold hands, thinking about what just happened.

"Will Adam be ok?" Her soft worried voice makes me smile and I nod. "I'll make sure of it."

"And us?" She sounds nervous which I hate and I pull her hard against me and say fiercely, "I will do everything in my power to keep you safe."

She hesitates and I pull her face to mine and see the anxiety in her eyes and I say firmly, "I'm afraid things have changed."

"In what way?" She bites her lip nervously and I groan. "I'm not letting you go, ever. You now have a life sentence with me because the thought of you leaving is not one I'm ever going to face."

"You're a bit sure of yourself, aren't you?"

A little of the old fire returns, accompanied by a soft smile, and my heart settles. "I am."

"What if I don't want to stay, I do have a life, you know?"

"Oh yes, I forgot, what was his name, Santa something?"

"Kenny." She giggles, and the sound of it is something I would pay all my billions to hear again.

"That's right, Kenny Santa. Maybe you should tell your sister about him."

"I already have."

"She obviously thinks he sounds like a deadbeat; we have that in common at least."

"Why do you say that?"

"Because she is trying to set you up with a fucking dentist. What's the matter, doesn't she trust your judgment?"

"No." She grins wickedly. "You see, I've got a track record of choosing the wrong man. Heartbreakers, fuck boys and men with no morals or standards. Men who cheat, men who lie, and men who treat me like shit. Maybe she's staging an intervention for my own good because I can't be trusted to choose my own destiny."

"Then allow me to choose it for you."

I lower my lips to hers and love the way they feel against mine. Like coming home, perfection and every happy ending in history. She moans against my lips and I feel my cock throbbing with an urgent need and yet she's been through so much today, only a bastard would force her into something she's not ready for.

"Fuck me, Lucas." Apparently, nobody told Ella that and with a feral growl, I push her robe from her body and lower my lips to taste her neck. I suck and love the moans that escape from her luscious mouth and as I lower her down onto the bed, she pushes my own robe from my shoulders and says with an urgency I love, "I need you inside me right now."

"Now who's the one calling the shots?"

I laugh as her legs wrap around my waist and she growls, "Stop talking and start fucking."

"Your wish is my command, my queen."

As I thrust inside the woman I love, I feel so many emotions it surprises me. I never knew it could be so good, a meeting of minds, souls and dreams. The king has found his queen, and she is magnificent. As I climax with an intensity I've never felt before, her own orgasm meets mine and we come down from the glorious high together. Lucas and Ella will become the Casino King and Queen, gambling royalty that will reign for a very long time, and now it's important we get to the bottom of the reason that brought us together.

This hasn't ended, it's just the beginning but one thing's for sure, I'm doing it with Ella by my side.

As I pull out, I stare into her gorgeous eyes and see the pure love shining out and say with more feeling than I've felt before, "I love you, Ella Quinn, will you marry me?"

I already know my answer as her lip quivers and her eyes burn brightly. "I thought you'd never ask."

As we kiss to cement the deal, I don't think I've ever been this happy in my life. From out of darkness came so much light it blinds me, and as I contemplate a life with my soul mate, I offer a vow to make her the happiest woman alive.

EPILOGUE

ELLA

*I*t doesn't seem fair that I can feel so happy when Adam is in hell. Just looking into his haunted eyes makes my heart shatter and thinking of how his wife met her end is a nightmare that will probably never go away. He has retreated into his own dark thoughts and thrown himself into business, and Lucas is keen to do anything he can to help him through the darkest period of his life.

So, where Lucas once lived here in his cavernous apartment alone, he now has two extra guests that appear to be here for some time and I am not arguing with that.

Through all this madness has come happiness, and I am fiercely protective of that.

ONE WEEK later to the day, I sit nervously beside Lucas in his office, facing the men who still make me question my own sanity.

Ryder King is sitting opposite Lucas, who sits beside me holding my hand. I don't think I've spent one minute alone since the party because he can't bear to let me out of his sight.

Beside Ryder is the man who will forever feature in my nightmares; the man who hauled Penelope off me and abducted me from the airport what feels like light years ago. The tattoo of the cobra that snakes up his arm reminds me what a killer looks like, although he wasn't the one who pulled the trigger, apparently.

Today's meeting is an important one judging by the looks on their faces and I can tell that Lucas is on edge, which makes *me* on edge.

Ryder sighs heavily and fixes us both with a dark look.

"Luckily for us all the operation has been a success. It didn't take long to uncover the person responsible, and once we discovered her intention, we set up surveillance on her. Tapped her phone and discovered her plan to finish the job at the brunch she arranged. We watched covertly and put a marker on her. Luckily, we have a recruit, a former sniper from the US military who apparently never misses his mark, and he was also the man responsible for taking out the woman who tried to kill us. We intercepted the text she sent you from Ella's phone and I knocked on the door as instructed and then stood to the side while I opened it and as she took aim and fired, Sawyer fired soon after."

He looks at me almost apologetically and shakes his head. "I'm sorry for what happened, but it had to be that way. We had our information, and she needed taking out. The clean-up crew has restored everything to what it was and disposed of the body. She will be explained as another suicide and the report will be buried and no questions ever asked. The operation now turns to the person responsible for setting the whole thing up which, as it happens, it turns out Penelope was working for someone in New York. She appears to have been recruited in Boston, probably up to twelve months ago.

When we started looking into your employees and friends, the trail led us to her door."

"So, she targeted Adam to get close to me." Lucas says angrily and Ryder nods.

I say sadly. "She told me it was always Lucas she was after. To get close to him in order to kill him. I asked her why, but she told me she was just being paid to do a job."

Ryder nods. "She was paid well. Penelope was not just a pretty face. She was a contract killer, and this wasn't her first rodeo. She was at the top of her game, and the person who recruited her obviously wanted a Trojan horse to roll in undetected. There were several transactions in an off shore account credited to her name. It was easy to trace, but that's where the trail ended. The funds came from an unnamed account that we are still working on, but the phone records gave us our only clue. The person sending them originated from a building in New York."

Ryder's expression is grim and there's a tense atmosphere in the room that feels ominous and Lucas snarls, "So, is it who we think it is?"

Ryder nods and for a moment they look at one another with devastation. I think I hold my breath as Lucas sighs. "So, what's the plan?"

"We go to New York."

Ryder's voice is blunt and unemotional, and Lucas shakes his head.

"Do you think he's involved?"

"What do you think?"

Lucas sighs and shakes his head. "No. I don't."

"What makes you so sure?"

Ryder leans forward and Snake looks interested as Lucas says roughly. "When you came here, you thought I was the man responsible for your own situation. I wasn't. I have a feeling Hunter is the next in line for whoever is trying to bring the organization down. It all adds up. Whoever wants us gone, is trying to blow us up from the inside. Set us against one another and let us finish the job they have started."

"My thoughts exactly."

"So, the business, the fact the stock exchange is throwing heat on my project, it must come from inside his office, but not necessarily from the man who sits at the head of it."

Ryder's expression is grim. "We need to discover what he knows. Tread carefully and not alert the person responsible that we're on his tail."

"Or her."

They look at me in surprise and I shrug, feeling a little bad that I have spoken up at all.

Lucas says softly, "What makes you think it's a woman?"

"Something Penelope said. She referenced a spider spinning a web and referred to it as her. It made me think because if I've got this right and please disregard anything I say if you think I'm way off mark but so far women have featured heavily in this. Maybe the person doing this is a woman."

Thinking of the story that Lucas told me of what happened after the coin left my shop, makes me feel cold inside. To think I played a small part in a staged murder makes me doubt every job I've ever carried out. Now there's this one and I shake my head.

"Penelope lured me into that room and was setting me up to take the blame for killing Lucas. She was going to shoot me too and frame me for his murder. At no point in this has a man ever been named, or even referenced. So, what makes you so sure it's not a woman?"

The men share a look and Ryder nods slowly. "You make a valid point."

Lucas squeezes my hand and smiles at me with such pride it makes my soul glow.

Lucas adds, "So what's your plan with Hunter and what do you need from us?"

"You carry on trying to save your business and looking into who could be leaking information in your own organization. It's still a possibility because someone is feeding this person, or organization their information. Keep a close eye on Adam, you never know…"

"It's not him." Lucas sounds angry and I smile to myself. I love how he loves his best friend. One hundred percent loyalty and an unwavering trust that gives me hope for us. Lucas may not let many people in, but when he does, it's for life. To be honest, I share his trust in Adam, although God knows why, just call it a sixth sense. Something in Adam's eyes tells me he's in the dark on this as much as Lucas.

Ryder nods. "I'll trust your judgment, but remember to trust nobody and suspect everybody until this mess is solved."

Lucas says roughly, "So, I repeat, what's your plan concerning Hunter?"

Ryder shares a look with his right-hand man.

"Well, Ella made a valid observation that had already crossed my mind."

Snake coughs beside him and Ryder rolls his eyes. "Ok, Snake's mind."

He grins as Snake growls, "Always tryin' to steal the credit."

Ryder grins and just seeing the two killers sitting before us sharing an obvious comradery that is built on years of trust, makes me warm toward them and feel fascinated by their lives.

Ryder continues. "We are sending someone in as we

speak. I'm not sure Hunter will be happy with our choice of protection, but shit happens."

Snake laughs and appears to be finding something very amusing, and Lucas says with interest. "Who is it?"

"Lexi Mackenzie."

Lucas laughs loudly and the two men opposite join in. I stare at them in confusion and Lucas turns to me and says with amusement.

"Lexi lived with Ryder and the Reapers for a while a few years back. She was like fire and ice and shook things up a little. She takes no shit but is wrapped in rainbows. She would knit you a scarf and then strangle you with it. A woman of conflicting souls, dark and light, and you never know which one you're getting."

Snake grins. "The perfect match for Hunter Blake."

"Who is Hunter Blake?"

Lucas laughs softly. "The King of Wall Street and the biggest bastard you'd be unfortunate to meet. A man with many enemies, and that's just his immediate family. The most ruthless bastard ever to rule the markets and one who is so cold the air he breathes out freezes around him."

"I'm not sure I like the sound of him."

I shiver just thinking of a man like that, and Ryder nods. "He doesn't want to be liked. The only thing he wants is money."

Lucas adds. "He is another member of our organization that makes sure the markets run to our advantage. He protects the country's investments and nothing gets past him. Whoever is doing this knows where to target because the problems I'm having in my business are all originating from the markets. Someone is casting doubt and causing them to shake. That will be giving Hunter the worst day at the office as he tries to discover the person responsible for that."

He turns to Ryder. "So, what can Lexi do?"

Ryder smirks. "She can get close to him. If there is a woman involved, she will soon discover their identity. Same if it's a man. One thing's for sure, whoever the person is, is using their own operatives to strike from the inside. We put Lexi there, and she reports back to me."

"And we get to watch Hunter meet his match. Hell, to be a fly on the wall."

The men laugh, but I'm still worried and say slightly nervously, "Are we all still in danger? I mean, surely we're still targets because they haven't got what they set out to do."

Ryder frowns. "Yes, unfortunately we need to close ranks and keep vigilant until this is ended. I'm sure you won't mind staying here until it is."

Lucas grabs my hand and growls. "You think I'm ever letting her go, even when it ends?"

The two men share a look and Ryder bursts out laughing. "Then it appears we have one man down already." He winks at me. "I'm sorry for your situation, I feel responsible."

Snake snorts beside him and Lucas shakes his head. "She has no complaints."

"Are you sure about that?" I inject ice into my voice and shake my head. "Always so cocky, Lucas, you really should work on that, it's so unattractive."

Laughing, Lucas turns to the men opposite. "She loves me, what can I say, I'm irresistible."

"Yeah, well, as I said, I'm sorry for your situation darlin'" and if you ever need rescuing, I'll send in a team."

Ryder winks and I giggle as Lucas rolls his eyes and as the men stand, Ryder holds out his hand which Lucas shakes warmly.

"I'll be in touch."

As they turn to leave, I can only wonder what will happen

next. It doesn't sound as if this is over anytime soon, and from the sounds of it, it's only just begun.

Lucas shows the men out, leaving me to think about what just happened. Despite the serious nature of this business, I wouldn't change a thing because it brought me to Lucas. We have a shot now, a chance of a good life - together. It has ended well for us, and I feel a little guilty about that. How can something so fantastic come out of something so destructive? It doesn't seem fair, but as Lucas heads back into the room and clicks the lock on the door, I feel the shiver of desire lighting a trail to my soul.

As he approaches me with dark intent, I feel the desire ripping my principles to shreds and as he rips off his tie, I lick my lips in anticipation.

My future is dark but the darker the sky, the brighter the stars shine and Lucas Emiliano is the deeper shade of darkness that makes my light burn so brightly, I am blinded to anything else.

So, I step into the darkness and know I am home, with him, the man destiny always had in her sights for me and I have no complaints about that.

~

CARRY on reading Break a King
The story continues…..

Learn More

Have you read book 1 in the series?
Catch a King.

Sawyer

I came to catch a killer. I found her.

A woman with so much sass wrapped in a body that will be my downfall.

She thinks she hates me, but hate doesn't look at me like that.

Beautiful, strong and brave but her loyalty lies with another.

She is to be auctioned and my brother is the only bidder.

Then I discover the truth. She was brought here for a reason.

My family will use her to bring our father's killer down.

Will I betray my own family to save her life?

Millie

It was hate at first sight.

I went undercover to find a killer. I found him.

When he looks at me, I'm a hot mess. I don't want to react to him; I don't think I even like him, but my body has other ideas.

Dark flashing obsidian eyes rip the breath from my body and leave me burning inside.

The scowl on the face of what can only be described as a god among men, is trying its best to scare the hell out of me and the fact this man is tall, broad and wrapped in leather and evil intent, sends a message straight to my soul.

My heart says he's going to break you, but you'll love him anyway.

DOWNLOAD CATCH a King

Before you go

Thank you for reading this story.
If you have enjoyed the fantasy world of this novel please would you be so kind as to leave a review on Amazon?

Join my closed Facebook Group

Stella's Sexy Readers

Follow me on Instagram

Stay healthy and happy and thanks for reading xx

CARRY on reading for more Reaper Romances, Mafia Romance & more.

Remember to grab your free copy of The Highest Bidder by visiting stellaandrews.com.

MORE BOOKS

Books by Stella Andrews

Standalone

The Highest Bidder (Logan & Samantha)

Rocked (Jax & Emily)

Bad Influence (Max & Summer)

Deck the Boss

Twisted Reapers

Daddy's Girls (Ryder & Ashton)

Twisted (Sam & Kitty)

The Billion Dollar baby (Tyler & Sydney)

Bodyguard (Jet & Lucy)

Flash (Flash & Jennifer)

Country Girl (Tyson & Sunny)

The Romanos

The Throne of Pain (Lucian & Riley)

The Throne of Hate (Dante & Isabella)

The Throne of Fear (Romeo & Ivy)

Lorenzo's story is in Broken Beauty

Beauty Series

Breaking Beauty (Sebastian & Angel) *

Owning Beauty (Tobias & Anastasia)

Broken Beauty (Maverick & Sophia) *

Completing Beauty – The series

Five Kings

Catch a King (Sawyer & Millie) *

Slade

Steal a King

Break a King

Reasons to sign up to my mailing list.

A reminder that you can read my books FREE with Kindle Unlimited.

Receive a monthly newsletter so you don't miss out on any special offers or new releases.

Links to follow me on Amazon or social media to be kept up to date with new releases.

Grab your free copy of The Highest Bidder as a thank you for signing up to my newsletter.

Opportunities to read my books before they are even released by joining my team.

Sneak peeks at new material before anyone else.

stellaandrews.com

Follow me on Amazon

Printed in Great Britain
by Amazon